Welcome to this month's collection of Harlequin Presents! At this festive time of year, why not bring some extra sparkle and passion to your life by relaxing with our brilliant books!

This month, Julia James brings you *Bedded, or Wedded?* Lissa's life has too many complications, but she just can't resist ruthless Xavier's dark, lethal sexuality. In *The Greek Tycoon's Pregnant Wife* by Anne Mather, Demetri needs an heir, but before he divorces Jane, he'll make love to her one last time. In *The Demetrios Bridal Bargain* by Kim Lawrence, Mathieu wants a wife of convenience, and grooming wild Rose in the marital bed will be his pleasure! Sharon Kendrick brings you *Italian Boss, Housekeeper Bride*, where Raffaele chooses his mousy housekeeper, Natasha, to be his pretend fiancée! If you need some help getting in the holiday mood, be sure not to miss the next two books! In *The Italian Billionaire's Christmas Miracle* by Catherine Spencer, Domenico knows unworldly Arlene isn't mistress material, but might she be suitable as his wife? And in *His Christmas Bride* by Helen Brooks, Zak is determined to claim vulnerable Blossom as his bride—by Christmas! Finally, fabulous new author Jennie Lucas brings you *The Greek Billionaire's Baby Revenge,* in which Nikos is furious when he discovers Anna's taken his son, so he vows to possess Anna and make her learn who's boss! Happy reading, and happy holidays from Harlequin Presents!

Kathryn Ross

TAKEN BY THE TYCOON

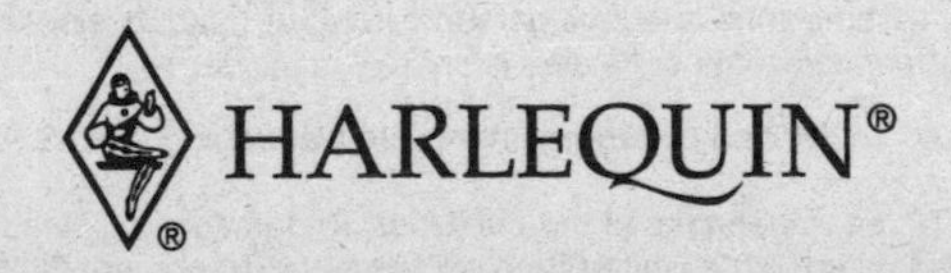

TORONTO • NEW YORK • LONDON
AMSTERDAM • PARIS • SYDNEY • HAMBURG
STOCKHOLM • ATHENS • TOKYO • MILAN • MADRID
PRAGUE • WARSAW • BUDAPEST • AUCKLAND

ISBN-13: 978-0-373-18882-6
ISBN-10: 0-373-18882-X

TAKEN BY THE TYCOON

First North American Publication 2007.

This edition published by arrangement with Harlequin Books S.A.

www.eHarlequin.com

Printed in U.S.A.

All about the author...
Kathryn Ross

KATHRYN ROSS was born in Zambia to an English father and an Irish mother. She was educated in Ireland and England, where she later worked as a professional beauty therapist before becoming a full-time writer.

Most of her childhood was spent in a small village in southern Ireland. She says it was a wonderful place to grow up, surrounded by the spectacular beauty of the Wicklow Mountains and the rugged coastline of the Irish Sea. She feels that living in Ireland sparked off her desire to write; it was so rich in both scenery and warm characters that it literally invited her to put pen to paper.

Kathryn loves to travel and seek out exotic locations for her books. She feels it helps her writing to be able to set her scenes against backgrounds she has visited. Traveling and meeting people also gives her great inspiration. That's how all her novels start—she gets a spark of excitement from some incident or conversation, and that sets her imagination working. Her characters are always a pastiche of different people she has met or read about, or would like to meet. She likes being a novelist because she can make things happen—well, most of the time, anyhow. Sometimes her characters take over and do things that surprise even her!

At present Kathryn is working on her next book, and can be found walking her dogs in the Lake District as she thinks about her plots.

CHAPTER ONE

THEIR eyes met across the boardroom table and out of nowhere Nicole could feel electricity in the air between them, so hot it almost sizzled. Hurriedly she looked away.

'So, as you can see, gentlemen,' she said as she tried to focus back on her notes, 'the figures are good. If there are no further complications the takeover should soon be complete and RJ Records will be ours.'

There was a ripple of applause around the long table and a lot of satisfied smiles. But Luke wasn't smiling. He was still looking at her with that gleam in his dark eyes as if he could read her mind and look directly into her very soul.

She wished he wouldn't look at her like that. It made her pulses race…it made her hot all over…it made her forget what she was thinking, what she was saying.

'So…' She shuffled the papers in front of her and forced herself to think businesslike thoughts. 'What we need to do now—'

'What we need to do now is adjourn this meeting,' Luke cut across her swiftly, his tone quietly commanding.

Nicole frowned, and was about to tell him that there were a few more important points to run through, but he was already pushing back his chair from the long polished table. 'Thank you for your attention, gentlemen, but I think with our goal in sight we all deserve an early finish tonight. We will reconvene early tomorrow morning.'

Nicole glanced surreptitiously at her watch. It was five-thirty. Not exactly early by normal standards, but compared with the hours they had been working for the last week this was a veritable half-day.

Everyone started to relax and follow the boss's lead, pushing their chairs back from the table. A babble of conversation broke out as the tension of the last few days was put aside. The whole office had been under pressure with work on the proposed takeover.

Nicole gathered her papers and put them back into her briefcase. Across the room she could see Luke chatting with Sandy, his PA. He was leaning against the window-sill, the panoramic view of the Miami skyline spread out behind him. But it wasn't the view outside that held Nicole's attention. It was the span of his shoulders in the charcoal-grey suit…the casual way he had pushed his jacket back to rest one hand against his white shirt, showing the taut lines of his narrow hips.

No man had a right to be as good-looking as her boss, she thought distractedly. Luke Santana was thirty-six and six-foot-two of sheer male perfection. His hair was thick, blue-black, and just a shade too long against his collar, and his eyes were so dark and intense that they seemed to slice into her. He was of Portuguese origin and you could see the continental lineage clearly, even if his accent was sometimes more mid-Atlantic. She liked the way he talked, with just an occasional hint of a Portuguese accent, and she liked the way he looked. In fact just glancing at him made her stomach tighten in a strange kind of way. But she was fighting that… In fact she was getting better at dealing with it, she told herself firmly as she turned her attention away from him. At least she was able to maintain a brisk, businesslike veneer around him—even if he made her heart speed up to the rate of an engine in overdrive.

A fellow colleague stopped to have a word with her and then she turned to leave. Luke was standing between her and the door now.

She pushed a strand of long chestnut hair back from her face and tried not to notice how his eyes flicked over her, taking in her slender figure in the white blouse and black pencil skirt.

'The deal seems to be coming together nicely, Nicole,' he drawled.

'Yes, I think we're making good progress.'

He nodded, before adding casually, 'However, there are a few points I think we should clarify, and one figure that I'd especially like to go over again in detail.'

Nicole's green eyes narrowed on him. She had been meticulous in her calculations…how could he not be completely satisfied? 'Which figure were you thinking of?'

'Don't worry about it now. Just make sure you are in here bright and early tomorrow.'

His tone held an abrasive edge, but she was kind of used to that. When Luke wanted something he wanted it then and there. Patience wasn't one of his virtues.

She nodded. 'Of course, boss.'

There was a slightly sardonic gleam in his eye now as he looked at her. 'See you tomorrow, Nicole,' he said.

She smiled and headed for the door.

The corridor outside was silent; she stepped into the lift to head back up to her office and collect her bag.

Before she reached her floor, her mobile rang.

'So, your place or mine?' an arrogant male voice demanded.

Her boss's cool, confident tones made a shiver of excitement race through her. 'I'm not sure I've got time to see you tonight,' she teased huskily. 'I've got figures to redo.'

'So have I...one figure in particular.' Nicole could hear the amusement in Luke's voice, but she could also hear the heat of desire. 'I'll be round at your place in half an hour.'

'Make it three quarters of an hour,' she said, thinking that she wanted time to get ready for him. 'I'll make us something to eat if you like?'

There was a silence at the other end of the phone, covered only by the distant babble of conversation from the boardroom. It was no wonder Luke was a bit surprised. She had never offered to cook for him before. Nicole frowned, surprised by the offer herself. Why had she said that? This was a strictly carnal affair—yes, OK, sometimes he took her out to eat, but that was in the impersonal surrounds of an expensive restaurant, and usually a restaurant where they wouldn't bump into anybody they knew. A home-cooked meal sounded somehow a little...cosy.

'OK, but I'd better warn you...I'm ravenous.' He said the words in a low, rasping tone and she had an immediate mental image of him arriving at her apartment and ripping her clothes off. That was what usually happened. Their time together was always wildly seductive...absolutely frenzied. Just thinking about it made all her senses reel with anticipation.

'I gather you are not talking about food now?' she said with a laugh.

'Got it in one.'

She could hear somebody talking to him in the background.

'Got to go,' he said swiftly. 'See you later.'

Nicole hung up with a frown. Why had she offered to cook for him? She wasn't a particularly domesticated person.

The lift doors opened and she walked through to her office. It was a fabulous space, with its own private lounge area, and behind her desk the Miami coastline sparkled clear and beautiful, like a jewel in the September sunshine. When the Santana Record Company had offered her a transfer out here eighteen months ago she had grabbed the opportunity with both hands. She had been delighted to leave London with its painful memories and start afresh.

During her time in America Nicole had dedicated herself entirely to her work, and it had paid off. Six months ago she had earned herself the position of Contracts Manager. It was no mean achievement at thirty-one. A record label like Santana was part of a hard-hitting business, and in order to rise so high she'd had to brazen it out in the boardroom, pretending to be the cool, invincible, perfectionist Ms Connell. It still stunned her that she had succeeded to convince people that this was the true her. Sometimes she found it amusing that her diminutive five-foot-five slender frame could be in command of anyone.

Everything had been going well. After a painful divorce it had suited her to put work first and relationships second. She had liked the fact that she only had an occasional date. She didn't want to get involved with anyone, had liked keeping everything uncomplicated. And then five months ago Luke Santana had flown into town. He'd been in Europe for the last eighteen months, and apparently they'd only narrowly missed meeting each other in the London office; she'd left for America the day before he arrived. Now he had returned to Miami to negotiate the takeover of another rival record company, RJ Records, and he had chosen Nicole to assist him. Suddenly life had veered off track.

Having an affair with the boss was probably not smart, and she had desperately tried to fight the attraction she felt for him. But from the first moment she had walked into his office and their eyes had met a sort of madness had descended on her.

'Hi, Nicole,' he had said easily as he stood up to shake her hand. 'I've been hearing great things about you.'

Nicole had heard things about him as well; she had heard that he was a ruthless entrepreneur who put the business of making money above everything else. According to the *New York Times* he bought and sold companies as if life was a game of Monopoly. Sometimes he kept the businesses and built them up; sometimes he just ruthlessly tore them apart in a game of asset-stripping. Luckily for her job, his record company was one that he was intent on building up.

Another thing she had heard about Luke Santana was that he had never married and, according to the gossips, had broken more women's hearts than there were days in the year. She had reminded herself of all those things as she had felt tingles of awareness just from his handshake. And because she had been determined to keep her distance she had made sure that around him she was extra cool and businesslike.

Luke had seemed to find this amusing, and a bizarre game of cat and mouse had ensued for a few weeks. The frostier she was, the more charming he became. He hadn't come on to her, in fact he hadn't done anything that could be considered improper…and yet there'd been a sizzling undercurrent that had grown stronger by the day. She'd tried everything to keep her distance—dressed in overly severe suits, scraped her hair back from her face, a sardonic disapproval when he had tested her knowledge of the business to the hilt. She had even told herself that she didn't like him very much—told herself and other people that he was overbearing and far too sure of himself.

But the tension between them—whatever it was—had just seemed to build and build. Then, during a late meeting of the board, her hand had accidentally brushed against his and the feeling had been electric. Such a trivial thing, and yet she'd hardly been able to think straight for the rest of the meeting. Later Luke had accompanied her back to her office to pick up some papers.

'You were very quiet tonight,' he said.

'Well, I've got a lot on my mind.' She found the papers in double-quick time. 'There you are,' she said as she handed them across. 'You'll find everything in order.'

'Yes, I'm sure I will. So, do you fancy having dinner with me some time?' he asked.

'To discuss these papers?'

He shook his head. 'No, to discuss this…'

Then he had kissed her.

The memory of that steamy kiss was enough to make her go hot inside now.

One moment she had been cool and reserved, the next she had melted like an ice-cube in the desert.

He had made love to her right here in her office, and it had been wild and incredible. Never in her life had she experienced such passion! Afterwards there had been a moment when she had been horrified by what she had done—especially when she remembered that he had been prepared for sex and had had a condom with him. But then he had kissed her so tenderly that the feeling had turned to elation.

She had been bewildered by her reaction, had reminded herself that she was a career girl who put emotional entanglements second.

The thought had made her pull away from him. 'I hope you are not going to read anything into this,' she said as she hurried to straighten her clothes and cover her nakedness. 'I've really no inclination to get involved with you. I've no time for a relationship right now.'

It was probably a stupid thing to say to a man like Luke. And certainly when she looked over at him he seemed somewhat amused.

'That suits me fine,' he drawled. 'I'm not cut out for relationships, Nicole.'

'Good. Well, we'll just forget all about this, then…shall we?' Somehow she managed to sound cool and composed, but really she was far from it. All she could think about was getting out of there. She had never felt more embarrassed in her life.

'I don't think so!' His voice was firm as he reached to take her hands away from the buttons on her blouse. 'I'm not finished with you yet, Ms Connell.' There was a playful, husky growl to his words, and she thought for one wild moment that he wanted to make love to her all over again… What was even more worrying was the fact that she wouldn't have been averse to the idea. But he was merely adjusting her clothing, refastening the buttons that she had mistakenly fastened crookedly. The touch of his fingers against her body was erotic.

'I suggest that we have an affair,' he said calmly. 'No complications, no strings…just perfect sex.'

And for the last few months that was what they'd had. So far they had managed to keep it a secret, so that it wouldn't complicate things at work. In public they were cool and deferential, but in private… Well, in private their affair was so hot it was on fire.

Nicole had never had a liaison like it before. Casual sex was something she had never indulged in. But then she'd had five years in a deeply committed relationship with her husband, and that had ended badly, so she told herself there was no harm in having a little fun. She was a thirty-one-year-old woman, for heaven's sake, and these were modern times.

Nicole's secretary, Molly, came into the room and put some letters on her desk. 'I didn't expect to see you back from that meeting so soon!' she said in surprise.

'Luke called a halt to proceedings and declared an early finish.'

'Wow! He must be in a good mood.'

'Indeed.' Nicole smiled and reached for her bag. 'So I suggest you take advantage and finish now, Molly.'

'Great! I'll have time to go down to the florist and sort out my flowers.'

'Can't be long now to the big day?' Nicole perched

against the edge of her desk for a moment. She liked Molly, a bubbly twenty-five-year-old who was so much in love with her fiancé Jack that it warmed Nicole's heart just hearing about their plans. And in some ways it restored her faith in love as well…a faith that had been badly shaken when her husband had walked out on her.

'Five weeks on Saturday.' Molly's eyes sparkled with happiness. 'In fact…' Molly disappeared back into her own office and then returned a minute later with an embossed envelope. 'I may as well give you your invitation now,' she said with a smile. 'I was going to post it, but I'm on the last minute getting them out anyway.'

'Thanks, Molly.' Nicole opened the envelope and looked down at the pretty card with two hearts interlinked by a gold wedding band on the front. Inside, the invitation was made out to 'Nicole and partner'.

Her first thought was that there was no way she could turn up accompanied by Luke. And then something strange happened…the knowledge seemed to sow a seed of sadness inside her.

With a frown, she pushed the feeling away. What on earth was the matter with her? Her relationship with Luke was just what she wanted, she told herself firmly as she put the invitation into her bag.

Twenty minutes later Nicole was pulling up outside her apartment in her red sports car, laden with bags from the local store. She had rethought her offer to cook for Luke and decided to stop off and buy some appetisers instead—maybe they could have them in bed together later. The idea had grown as she'd walked around the store, and she had got a little carried away and bought champagne and caviar and all sorts of goodies. She felt quite excited as she headed for the lifts. The thought of a whole evening with Luke was blissful.

She had fifteen minutes to spare as she hurried through her front door. Throwing her purchases into the fridge, she headed for the bedroom and had a quick shower before putting on some sexy cherry-red lingerie and a wraparound dress in a matching colour. There was just time to pull a brush through her long chestnut hair and apply some lipstick.

She studied herself for a moment in the mirror. Her eyes were wide and sparkling with anticipation, and there was a healthy glow to her skin. Anybody would think she was in love. The light-hearted thought flicked through her brain and suddenly she froze.

She wasn't in love! She couldn't be in love! It was against all the rules. This was an affair…it was casual sex with a capital C—no strings, no commitment, and certainly no mention of the L word.

So why did her heart go into overdrive when he so much as looked at her? a small voice asked. Why had she felt unhappy that they couldn't attend Molly's wedding as a couple?

The front doorbell rang and she whirled around, her senses pounding guiltily as if she had been caught out in some illegal or immoral act.

She told herself that she was imagining things as she headed to open the door. There was no way she had fallen in love with Luke Santana. She wasn't that brainless. She knew there was no way he wanted a meaningful relationship. One hint of that and he would be heading for the hills at double speed. And anyway, hadn't she promised herself after her divorce that she wasn't going to do love again? It only led to heartache. She liked this casual no-strings approach. Really, she could take him or leave him.

Feeling a little better, she swung the door open.

Luke was leaning against the door-frame. He was wearing the same grey suit he had worn in the office, and he was loosening his tie as if it were cutting into him. There was no other way to describe him other than overwhelmingly sexy. Nicole felt her heart doing its usual dip down towards her stomach.

'Sorry I'm a bit late.' He smiled at her, with that lazy smile that seemed to warm the darkness of his eyes. 'I got caught on the phone.'

Take him or leave him? Who was she trying to kid? she thought distractedly. She was crazy about him…and deeply in love.

'Are you OK?' he asked as he stepped past her.

'Yes, of course.' She pulled herself together sharply. This was a disaster…what the hell was she going to do?

CHAPTER TWO

'WOULD you like a drink?' Nicole headed for the kitchen. 'I've got champagne cooling.'

She opened up her fridge and the array of party food seemed to mock her. She didn't feel like celebrating any more.

Why hadn't she seen the signs that she was falling for him? she wondered. She felt as if someone had just taken the blinkers from her eyes and for the first time in weeks she had clear vision. The signals had all been there, but she had either been too preoccupied or too damn silly to see them. There was the breathless feeling when she was with him, the lack of appetite when she was not. The aching disappointment when he didn't spend the whole night with her after they made love.

And now there was the sudden feeling that she wanted to get to know him on a deeper level. Well, she wasn't going to give in to those feelings. She snatched up the bottle of champagne.

'Champagne? Are we celebrating?' He was at the doorway, watching her.

'Not especially, since the deal for RJ isn't settled yet.' She brought her thoughts firmly back towards work.

'You look lovely, by the way,' he said softly as she walked over to get some glasses.

'Thank you.' She looked over at him and felt herself melt. Luke had a way of looking at her and undressing her with his eyes. He had been doing it in the boardroom this afternoon. And there was something so profoundly sensual about it that it sent her blood pressure soaring. If anyone else had been so forward she might have been annoyed, but with him it really, really turned her on.

All she could think about now was how much she wanted him.

'Shall I open that bottle for you?' He moved to stand behind her, and before she could answer him he had taken the champagne from her hand and was uncorking the bottle. His arms were around her shoulders and she could smell the deliciously provocative scent of his cologne, could feel his body hard and lean against hers. She closed her eyes on a wave of intense desire.

'There.' The cork whizzed out of the bottle and some of the froth sprayed over them. They both laughed, and he put the bottle down to place his hands on her waist and kiss the side of her face. 'I've been wanting to touch you all day,' he murmured.

'Me too…' She leaned back against him and reached up to run her fingers through the dark silkiness of his hair.

His hands moved from spanning her small waist to run upwards over the curves of her body. Immediately her breasts responded to his touch and became hard with arousal. 'You know, you add a whole new and exciting element to opening a bottle of champagne, Nikki.' He murmured the words huskily against her ear and she turned around and melted into his arms.

He liked the way she did that, liked the way she responded to his touch and fitted against him, sinuously inviting yet curvaceously warm. When he had watched her in the boardroom today he had imagined this moment. He had listened as she talked about facts and figures with that brisk efficiency of hers, and he had taken infinite pleasure in the knowledge that later he would be the one to ruffle her calm, cool exterior and arouse her to fever pitch. She was extremely sexy…biddable in the bedroom, yet a force to be reckoned with in the workplace. He found that fascinating, and he intended to explore every inch of her delectable foxy body right here…right now…

His lips ground down against hers, hard and punishing, and she kissed him back with a passion of equal strength. He liked that too.

'Sex is so good between us…' He murmured the words huskily as he trailed red-hot kisses like darts of fire down the side of her neck.

Nicole agreed with him, but inside there was suddenly a traitorous little voice cutting through the waves of passion and mocking her. *You want this to be more than just good sex…*

She pulled away from him, desperately trying to close those thoughts out.

'Are you OK?'

'Fine!' She turned towards the counter-top for a moment. 'I just thought we'd have that drink.' Quickly she rallied herself. She didn't want to ruin their time together with these irrational thoughts. When she looked back at him, she flashed him a provocative look from smouldering green eyes. 'It would be a shame to let it go to waste after the trouble you took to open it.'

One dark eyebrow rose mockingly. 'If you say so…but I did have other things on my mind.'

'So I noticed.' She smiled, then turned away from him. *Sex* was on his mind, while meantime she was filled with these crazy feelings of love. She needed to get rid of them, and quickly. But it was like Pandora's box: the lid was off and all sorts of unwelcome feelings were pounding through her body with insistent force.

Nicole's hand wasn't quite steady as she poured the drink. Luckily Luke didn't seem to notice. He was reaching past her to pick up a designer box that was sitting by the microwave.

'Nice tie,' he said with approval as he took a look inside.

She glanced over and her heart sank. Oh hell! That was another thing she had done…bought him a gift…for no reason at all.

'Yes, isn't it?' It had been very expensive too. Nicole was really thankful now that she had been too busy to give it to him. She had her pride, and she didn't want him to guess that she was falling for him…that would be excruciatingly embarrassing. If he got one hint of her thoughts he would probably pull the plug on their relationship. After all, he'd made his feelings on commitment abundantly clear on more than one occasion. He had even gone so far as to tell her once that marriage and babies were certainly not what he wanted in life. His work came first.

'Who is it for?'

'Just a friend. It's his birthday next week,' she improvised quickly as she turned to pass him his drink. OK, there was no real reason why he should guess what was in her heart just from one gift, she told herself sensibly. But she wasn't going to take any chances. Because the strange thing was that now she had realised the truth it suddenly seemed so glaringly obvious.

He held the glass up and touched it against hers. 'Cheers,' he said softly.

'Cheers.' She took rather too deep a swallow of the champagne and bubbles tickled her nose. This drink was like their relationship, she thought: very pleasurable, but all froth and no real substance. She would do well to remember that if she wanted to continue to enjoy it.

'I thought the board meeting went well today.' Deliberately she turned the conversation back towards the safety of work.

'Yes, you did a good job,' he said quietly. 'I was impressed.'

'I know.' She looked at him teasingly. 'Yet you told me there were further points to clarify and…how did you put it?…one figure in particular that you needed to go over?'

'And I intend to go over it…in fine detail…any moment now…' He drawled the words provocatively. 'But I was playing things carefully. I didn't want people to overhear, put two and two together and realise we are sleeping together.'

He always referred to them as just 'sleeping together'. It had never bothered her before, but today it made her heart thud painfully against her chest. Even the term 'sleeping together' was a bit of an exaggeration for what they had. In reality they did little sleeping, as Luke usually left after they'd made love.

'That would never do,' she said lightly.

'Never,' he agreed, with a wry gleam in his eyes.

It had been Nicole's idea to keep the affair a secret; she really didn't want to be the subject of office gossip. Luke, on the other hand, found the secrecy amusing. It was a game he seemed to enjoy playing.

'Speaking of which…' he continued softly. 'I know you said you'd make dinner, but I think we should put that on hold for a while.'

'Oh, I changed my mind about dinner,' she said airily. 'I thought we'd have nibbles instead…'

'That sounds good…' He put his glass down and then reached to take hers from unresisting fingers. 'I'm all for nibbles.' As he spoke he brushed her hair away from her face and then leaned in closer to nibble gently at her ear-lobe. The sensation was deliciously intoxicating.

'Now, where were we?' he murmured huskily, and she felt his hands moving down over the curves of her body with bold possession. 'You know, I don't think I can wait one minute longer for you.'

The wraparound dress was easily pushed to one side and his hands found the naked heat of her body. Nicole closed her eyes on a wave of desire. She didn't think she could wait one minute longer for him either. She had wanted him all afternoon. Had longed for the people around them to disappear so she could just melt into his arms.

His lips found hers in a hard, yet sensationally passion-ate kiss. She kissed him back, loving the warm feeling that melted through her body.

Wrapping her arms around his neck, she lost herself in his caresses. His tongue was inside her mouth now, plundering her sweet softness.

Then his kisses became even more intense, his hands fiercely possessive. She allowed him to untie her dress completely and it dropped to the floor. Suddenly Luke was pulling back from her, and his gaze raked over the slender curves of her body in the sexy underwear. 'Hell, but you're beautiful, Nicole.' He reached a hand out and trailed it softly over the edge of her lacy bra. Immediately her body responded to him; she could feel her breast tightening with need.

It was only four days since they had last made love, yet her body felt starved of his…it was almost as if a fever had taken hold of her and she ached all over.

As he pulled her bra down, exposing the creamy curves of her figure, she felt every sinew of her body glowing and alive with need. His lips moved to nuzzle in against her neck as his hands caressed her curves, then his mouth moved lower, following his hands.

Just as she felt she was going to explode with need he picked her up and carried her through to the bedroom.

They sank down onto her double bed and she started to feverishly unfasten the buttons of his shirt. 'I want you so much,' she said, her voice incoherent with need.

The shirt was discarded and she stroked her fingers lovingly over the smooth breadth of his shoulders. He had a fabulous body…finely tuned, and toned like an athlete's. He was slowly kissing her all over. She loved the way he could be so masterful in the bedroom, yet so incredibly tender at the same time. Her need for him was building up to fever pitch, and as his lips returned to hers again the passion became wilder, less controlled. He pulled her closer and suddenly he was inside her, taking her with hard, driving thrusts yet at the same time stroking her breasts with gentle possession.

The sensations he aroused in her were overwhelmingly intense, but she tried not to give in to them, tried to prolong the pleasure. But the ache of need was building until she felt she couldn't stand it any more. As his lips nuzzled against her she hit dizzying heights, and together their passion exploded into a million splintering pieces of sheer pleasure.

'Wow!' It was all she could say. She was out of breath and her skin was damp against his.

He gave a low laugh and rolled over to lie beside her. 'You can say that again!' There was a gleam of warm amusement in his eyes as he looked across into her eyes. 'That was perfect.'

Nicole wished she could say the same. Yes, she felt physically sated, but there was a raw ache inside her that wouldn't go away… It was the ache of knowing how much she loved him and how futile that love was. This man would never be hers. Trying to claim Luke would be a bit like trying to catch a tiger by the tail. The knowledge hurt unbearably.

For a while they just lay there without speaking.

Her eyes moved over his face. It was such an arrestingly handsome face, she thought. She noticed how his jaw was square and determined, how there was a slight dimple in the hollow of his chin, and how already there were the beginnings of a dark shadow along the olive smoothness of his skin.

Luke reached out a hand and pulled her a little closer to him. She allowed herself to cuddle in against him and he kissed the side of her face. She kissed him back, and then suddenly he was pulling her underneath him and they were making love all over again.

'Where do you get your energy?' she asked him breathlessly when she finally lay exhausted against his sprawled body.

'I don't know. Maybe it's something to do with my Mediterranean roots,' he said playfully. He pushed her silky hair back from her face and looked down at her. She liked the way his dark eyes were flecked with gold, and how they crinkled slightly at the edges when he smiled.

She tried to commit this moment—and him—to memory. And for a precious few seconds she snuggled against him and tried to pretend that they belonged together…that he was all hers. His hand ran down the long length of her spine and then curved around her waist, pulling her even closer.

The shrill ring tone of his mobile phone suddenly broke the relaxed mood. Nicole groaned inwardly and wanted to tell him to ignore it. But she knew better. Work always came first with Luke.

As she had known he would, he reached across and answered it immediately.

'Oh, hi, Amber—how is it going?' Within a second he had pulled completely away from her and sat up in the bed. 'Did you get the figures from Drew? Good. So it's on target, then?'

Nicole lay against the pillows, watching him. It never ceased to amaze her how fast Luke could switch from the warmth of lovemaking to the cool practicality of business. Amber was one of his top accountants who had been at his New York office for the last week.

She wished the outside world would go away… She wished that Luke would look at her and suddenly realise he couldn't live without her…

Now she was being ridiculous! Angry with herself, she tried to close out thoughts like that.

Luke finished his phone call and looked over towards her. 'I'm sorry, Nicole. I'd really better go. I need to do some work at home for the New York office.'

She noticed how his tone was brisk and businesslike. So much for the outside world going away, she mocked herself wryly. So much for her romantic plans for a long evening together and a picnic in bed. She should have known better.

'OK.' With a supreme effort she matched her tone to his. 'I'll make you a coffee while you shower.'

'That would be great, thanks.'

Nicole put on her dressing gown and went through to the kitchen. She didn't really want coffee, but she felt she needed to do something to keep herself busy. Dwelling on this…attraction for Luke was doing her no good! When her marriage had broken up she had sworn she would never let any man get close enough to hurt her again. With determination she had put her life back together, and she had become fiercely independent…self-sufficient. If she gave in to these feelings for Luke now she would be undoing all her good work… breaking all her rules. She was going to have to pull herself together and get some control over her emotions.

When she returned to the bedroom, Luke was just coming out of the *en suite* bathroom. He had a towel wrapped low around his waist and he looked like a Greek god, all muscled perfection with a lean washboard stomach.

He smiled at her and it made her pulses quicken, made

all her firm resolutions waver. 'I made you that coffee,' she said brightly, putting it down on the bedside table.

'Thanks.'

He sat down next to her on the edge of the bed and she noticed how his hair was wet and slicked back, emphasising the lean contours of his face. She wanted to reach out and touch him.

Linking her fingers firmly around her mug of coffee, she forced herself not to, tried to distract her thoughts away from how attractive she found him.

Luke's glance fell on the wedding invitation she had left on the bedside table. 'What's this?' he asked casually as he reached to pick it up.

'Molly invited me to her wedding today.'

'Molly?' He frowned.

'My secretary,' she reminded him. 'You know—'

'Oh, yes…Molly. Attractive girl with blonde curly hair.'

'That's her.' Nicole nodded. She supposed he couldn't be expected to remember all his employees. It was a big firm…and not the only one he owned!

He opened the card. 'The invitation is for you and a partner. Who are you going to take?'

She shrugged. 'I haven't had time to think about it yet.'

'It could have been fun to go together.'

The nonchalant words cut through her. It would have been wonderful to spend time with him openly. 'But we need to keep our affair secret from people at work,' she murmured cautiously. 'Molly might be a bit shocked if we turn up together.'

'Yes, that's the problem.' He laughed. 'And we don't want to blow our little secret, do we? It's far too enjoyable.'

'Absolutely.' She forced herself to smile.

'It keeps things exciting and fun,' he added with a teasing grin.

'Yes, it does.' She took a deep breath and decided to test the water all the way. 'And…after all…it's not as if our relationship is serious, is it?…'

Luke nodded. 'I agree, Nicole. Things are just fine the way they are.'

'I think so too.' *Liar!* a little voice taunted her inside, and desperately she tried to ignore the raw feelings it stirred up.

He put the invitation down and took a sip of his coffee. 'Well, that's OK, then.'

Suddenly she wanted to say, *Actually, no, it's not OK.* But with difficulty she reined in the feeling. She had no right to feel upset. She had agreed right from the beginning that this was a no-strings affair. So she couldn't complain now just because she felt like moving the goalposts.

But the trouble was the more she thought about it, the more upset she felt. With determination, she fought down the feeling.

'So, who will you go to the wedding with?' Luke asked casually.

She shrugged. 'I might just go on my own,' she said airily. 'It can be quite good fun being unattached at a function. You meet more people.'

Luke put his coffee down. 'Well, as long as you come home alone I have no objection.'

The statement made her temper flare. He couldn't expect to have everything his own way! 'Oh, really?' She looked at him with a raised eyebrow. 'I think you'll find you've no right to object to *anything* I might do…'

'Uh-uh.' He shook his head and reached purposefully to take her coffee from her. 'I'll think you'll find I can register my objections very loudly.' Although his voice was playful, his hands were very serious as they moved over her body with firm possession.

And suddenly his lips crushed against hers with a vivid and almost aggressive passion. If he didn't care about her would he kiss her like this? she wondered dazedly. She tried to hold herself back and not surrender to him. But as Luke trailed a heated blaze of kisses down over her face and along the side of her neck she found herself winding her arms around his neck and giving herself up to the moment.

Now he was sliding her further down the bed. 'I thought you had to go and deal with work?' she said breathlessly.

'Yes, I should really go…but first I want you again.' He ripped her dressing gown off with determined hands. 'Right now you belong to me, Ms Connell.' His voice held an arrogant confidence, as did the touch of his hands against her skin as they slid possessively up along the naked slender curves of her hips and waist.

'On the contrary. I belong to no one but myself!' she said firmly, and she wriggled away from him a little.

He pulled her back easily, and a playful struggle ensued before he pinned her against the bed.

He said something to her in Portuguese. It sounded deliciously provocative.

'What did you say?' she murmured.

'I said we'd see about that, my little wildcat.' Luke's voice was teasing and his grip gentle, yet he held her without difficulty beneath him, both her wrists fastened behind her head with just one hand.

He looked down into her eyes and she loved the powerful feeling of intimacy and sensuality that suddenly spun between them.

'God, you are so beautiful…' he said huskily. Then he bent his head and kissed her with a passion that showed her exactly how easily he could stake his claim.

She kissed him back, and the play-acting was forgotten. Luke released his grip on her wrist and their fingers intertwined. His body was hard and possessive against her.

The intimacy between them was so tender, so…warm and loving, that Nicole couldn't equate it at all with the cool certainty that Luke had shown when he'd agreed that it meant nothing.

Since meeting him she had become more alive. He had reawakened her in every way. In fact even her husband hadn't made her feel like this! So how could it not be the real thing?

'You like that, Nikki, don't you?' He whispered the words against her ear.

Like? That was far too weak a word for what Nicole was feeling. She felt as if a burning volcano of need was stored inside of her. When he broke away from her briefly she thought for one horrible moment that he was stopping, but when she glanced around she found he was only reaching for a condom.

As he caressed her, she felt as if she were spinning further and further out of control. He was masterful with her, yet infinitely tender and he made her respond to him without inhibition. By the time he allowed her release from the wildness of her need she felt like crying with pleasure. And all she could do was just cling to him, because she was totally and utterly exhausted in every sense.

Luke watched her as she fell asleep in his arms. Her skin was flushed with heat and her hair was glossy around her shoulders. He allowed one hand to trail provocatively over the smoothness of her back and watched how she smiled in her sleep and cuddled a little closer.

Nicole had stirred a surprising feeling of possessiveness inside him, and that wasn't like him at all. He frowned as he thought about that feeling now. It had probably just been pure desire. He had to admit she turned him on with an incredible force.

And he had to admit that she intrigued him too. What made her tick? he wondered. What drove her?

Watching her in action at the office was a sight to behold. One moment she was provocative and sexy, and the next he'd glimpse this clear-thinking and tenacious woman who could pull off the most audacious of deals when the stakes were at their highest.

She was certainly tough, and she seemed to take emotional issues lightly—in fact she was very much on his wavelength in that respect. She didn't believe in getting bogged down in restrictive relationships, she was career-orientated. And yet at other times he thought he glimpsed an almost fragile vulnerability about her, and then it was gone, making him wonder if he'd imagined it.

When he'd taken her out to dinner the first time she'd told him she was divorced. She had only mentioned it fleetingly, yet he had seen that look in her eyes and noticed how she had quickly moved the conversation back towards the safety of work.

Was she as emotionally tough as she seemed? Or did she hide herself away behind a steely façade?

Luke frowned to himself as he suddenly realised that he was analysing her. Did it matter what motivated Nicole? This was just a light-hearted affair. They shared a lot of laughs, had the same sense of humour. For whatever reason she was a free spirit, like him, and that suited him just fine.

He glanced at his watch, irritated by his introspection. He needed to get his priorities in order—get back to his apartment and phone Amber to make sure the figures were correct on that contract for the New York office.

Very gently Luke eased himself away from Nicole, and, trying carefully not to wake her, he got out of the bed. She stirred a little, but settled back against the pillow without opening her eyes. Stealthily he got dressed. He was just looking around for a pen so that he could scribble a note for her when she opened her eyes.

'You're dressed!' She held the sheet against her body as she struggled to sit up.

'Sorry, I didn't mean to wake you.'

'That's OK.' She pushed the heavy fall of hair away from her face and tried to focus on him. 'Do you have to rush off?' Her voice was sleepy. 'You could stay and have something to eat if you want?'

'Sorry, honey, but you know I've got to go. I told you—I have to get back to my apartment and switch on my computer so I can go through those figures with Amber.'

'Yes, of course.' She drew in her breath and berated herself for asking him to stay. She should have known better. Just because he'd made love to her again it didn't mean he'd changed his mind about leaving. And anyway, this was what always happened…one moment he was curled up with her in bed, holding her tenderly, and the next he was racing to get back to a damn business problem. She'd used to tell herself that it didn't matter, that she didn't care...but she did!

I'm not going to put up with this any more, she thought suddenly. This isn't what I want. With difficulty she remained calm. This wasn't the moment for a confrontation. 'Another time, then,' she drawled.

'Yes, another time.' His eyes flicked lazily over her. It amused him that she was holding the sheet so tightly across her naked body...after all, he'd seen all there was to see.

'How about dinner tomorrow night?' he asked casually as he reached for his tie.

'Actually, I'm busy tomorrow night.'

He glanced over at her, surprised by the refusal. 'OK, we'll take a raincheck.'

'Yes...good idea.' She was sliding back down in the bed now. She stretched and the sheet fell a little lower, down over the curve of her breast.

Surprisingly, Luke found his body starting to respond to the lissom arch of her body, and suddenly he wanted to join her in the bed again. Forcibly he reached for his jacket.

'I hope you get those contracts sorted out.'

'Thanks.' Luke slung his jacket over his shoulder and looked over at her. 'And thanks for a great evening. I've enjoyed myself.'

Nicole couldn't find a light-hearted reply for that. Her heart was beating so loudly she felt it was filling the room with a noise like a bass drum.

'If you are busy tomorrow night we could always just meet up later?' he suggested lightly. 'Take up where we left off tonight?'

Meet up just for sex, in other words. Anger was pounding through her now. 'Actually, I'm going to be out with the girls until late tomorrow night,' she said coolly. In fact she had made no arrangements for tomorrow evening. But she was damned if she was going to make herself available just when it suited him.

He didn't seem to notice her frosty tone. 'OK. Well, we'll leave it until after the weekend, then.'

Nicole made no reply.

'I'll see you tomorrow morning in the office.'

'Bright and early,' she said with mock cheeriness.

He reached and ruffled the silky softness of her hair, and before she realised his intention he bent and kissed her full on the mouth in a sensual and provocative kiss that made her heart beat even faster.

'Bye, Nicole.'

'Bye.' She turned her head into the pillow as the door closed behind him, and then she was left with the silence of her apartment.

Their relationship was sexual and there would never be anything deeper than that between them. She either accepted that or walked away.

She bit down on her lip. As much as she wanted to accept the status quo, she knew now that she couldn't. Her true feelings for him wouldn't allow her. So tomorrow she would finish with him, she promised herself fiercely.

CHAPTER THREE

NICOLE was running late. She hadn't slept well at all. Her mind had been going over and over her time with Luke as she tried to analyse her situation. But analysing emotions was never a good idea…especially in the dead of night, she thought angrily as she straightened the bedclothes. The only thing she had achieved was a feeling of lethargy.

The drawer of the bedside table was open and a packet of condoms stared up at her. Luke was always very careful to use contraception. He had told her quite categorically that he didn't want her to get pregnant. What she hadn't been able to bring herself to tell him was that he had no need to worry about that. Nicole knew she *couldn't* get pregnant. She had longed for a baby when she was married, and she and her husband had tried for a long time to conceive without success. The fault had been found to lie with her, and the agony of the situation had been beyond compare. Ultimately she knew it was what had led to the break-up of her marriage.

She slammed the drawer shut. Yes, she did like the fact that Luke was responsible when it came to making love. But it was quite revealing that the only personal item that he ever left here was a packet of condoms.

When they had first started to sleep together she had suggested that he leave a few things here, like shaving gear and a change of clothes. It had seemed like a practical suggestion to her, and she supposed deep down she had been hoping that if he took her up on it he would stay around with her for longer. But he'd dismissed the idea immediately.

'There is no point, Nicole,' he had said in a matter-of-fact tone. 'My place is only fifteen minutes away. It is as easy for me to go back there.'

And she was losing sleep over the decision to finish with him! Annoyed with herself, Nicole reached to pick up her briefcase and cast a look at her reflection in the mirror. She was wearing a dark pinstripe suit that had a straight skirt teamed with a plain white blouse. Her dark chestnut hair fell in a gleaming curtain, framing her heart-shaped face, and she had done a good job with her make-up. At least she looked the part of the cool, composed businesswoman.

Ahead of her lay a busy day. She had to finish her presentation in the boardroom, and she needed to keep her wits about her and remember her priority was work.

Nothing else matters, she told herself fiercely. You can't rely on a man…you can only rely on yourself in the end. It was a lesson she'd learnt the hard way in the past, and she reminded herself of that fact now as she left for the office.

Her secretary was already in. 'Morning, Nicole. There is a stack of mail waiting for you on your desk,' she said cheerfully.

'Thanks, Molly.' Nicole walked through to her office, switched on her computer and logged in her password so she could check her e-mails. There was one from Luke; by the looks of things he'd sent it in the early hours of this morning.

Why don't you cancel whatever you are doing tonight and come round to my place for drinks? We can continue where we left things last night.

Hell, but he could be arrogant, she thought with a flash of annoyance. Did he think he only had to click his fingers and she'd come running?

She deleted the message without replying to it. Then she turned her attention to the rest of her business correspondence.

She had just finished reading her mail when another e-mail message arrived from Luke.

Morning, Nicole. Do you want to come up and have a coffee with me before we go in to this board meeting?

She wanted to ignore him, but she couldn't really; he was her boss. After a moment's hesitation she replied.

Good morning, Luke. Can't come up. I've got a few things to summarise before the board meeting. See you then.

A few seconds passed and a reply pinged onto the desk.

Just leave whatever you are doing.

Nicole frowned. She supposed that was a command! She sat drumming her fingers onto her desk. Well, if she was going to finish with him maybe now was as good a time as any. It was best to get it over with, she told herself firmly.

Picking up her briefcase, so that she was ready to go

straight to the board meeting afterwards, she headed up to the top floor.

Luke's PA waved her through towards the inner office with a smile. 'He's expecting you, Nicole.'

With a feeling of determination Nicole pushed open the door and went in. This was going to be difficult, but she was going to have to be strong, she told herself resolutely. When she'd got it over with she could take control of her life again.

Luke was sitting behind his desk, talking on the phone; he looked up and smiled at her, his eyes flicking over her slender figure with warm approval.

Immediately she felt her resolve starting to weaken.

'No, Thomas, it's not good enough,' he was saying firmly as he waved at Nicole to sit down in the chair opposite him. 'I won't be a moment,' he murmured, covering the mouthpiece.

She nodded, and tried to focus her attention on the room rather than on him. She'd always thought that Luke's office was more like a suite at a hotel than a place of work. He had everything up here: a lounge with a full bar area, even a walk-in closet with a few suits and shirts hanging up, and a large *en suite* bathroom with a shower and a Jacuzzi.

They had made love up here once. She remembered it now—the way he had undressed her and kissed her all over as he slowly, slowly turned her on to the point where she was just begging him to release her into blissful satisfaction.

Luke put down the phone, and swiftly she closed her mind on that. Memories like that didn't help at all right now.

'Sorry about that.' He smiled at her.

'That's OK.' She smiled back and tried very hard not to be distracted by how attractive he looked.

'And I'm sorry about having to leave so early last night,' he said.

There was a part of her that wanted to say, *You always leave early*… But she held back from that. She knew it would sound too possessive and too revealing, and she had her pride. So she just shrugged. 'I know that business comes first for both of us.' She was pleased at how cool and in control she sounded. 'Did you sort out the figures with Amber?'

'Yes…but we had to come into the office. We were at it until after midnight.'

At what? Nicole wondered distractedly. It didn't help to remember that Amber was a very attractive woman. Flame-haired and slender, with the most amazing blue eyes. *At work*, she told herself fiercely. And even if they hadn't been working it was none of her business. She was finishing with Luke…*remember*?

He got up from his chair and perched nearer to her on the edge of his desk. 'So, as we didn't get around to eating last night, can I make it up to you tonight?' he asked. 'I thought dinner at La Luna?'

La Luna was one of the best restaurants in the area. She had never been there because it was always booked up a long time in advance.

'No. I told you I couldn't make it tonight, Luke.' She brushed at an imaginary crease in her jacket.

'Well, that's a shame.'

Yes, it was. She wanted to accept the invitation; she wanted to forget this notion about finishing with him. If they went out for dinner he would take her home afterwards, and she would invite him in, and then… Swiftly she closed her mind to that. Every time she slept with him she was falling deeper and deeper under his spell, and it was a disaster. The relationship was going nowhere. She had to be strong.

'Actually there's something I need to say to you, Luke.' The words tumbled out hurriedly.

'And what is that?'

Nicole noticed how his tone of voice was huskily friendly.

Her eyes drifted over him, taking in the lightweight suit that looked so good on his broad-shouldered frame. He was wearing a blue shirt beneath, and it seemed to emphasise the almost blue-black intensity of his hair.

'Nicole?' His dark eyes seemed to slice straight through her.

This was one of the hardest things she had ever had to do. In order to take her mind off that fact, she stood up and put a little distance between them. If he touched her…if he kissed her…she would be lost.

'The thing is, this isn't working out, Luke.'

'What isn't working out?' He was half looking towards his computer as an e-mail arrived on screen.

'Us.'

'Us?' He frowned and looked back at her immediately.

'What we have together, Luke…you know…it's just not working.'

'What on earth are you talking about?' He smiled now, as if he thought she was joking. 'Of course it's working. What we have is fabulous.'

'Yes, it has been fabulous,' she admitted. 'But it's time for us to finish it.'

'Why would we finish something when we are both

still enjoying ourselves?' He looked genuinely perplexed. 'We've been having fun together, haven't we?'

'Yes.' She swept an unsteady hand through her hair. That was all she was to him, she reminded herself fiercely. A *bit of fun*. 'But it's run its course, Luke.'

'I don't think so.' He shook his head. 'The sex between us is as hot as ever. Yesterday you were as keen to get out of that boardroom and into bed as I was.'

'Yes.' She really didn't want to think about that right now. 'But now I just think it's time that we end it,' she said firmly.

He looked at her with a raised eyebrow and she could tell he still wasn't taking her seriously. 'Is this because I had to leave earlier than usual last night?'

'No, of course not.' She folded her arms in front of her body, trying to keep herself focused.

'It is, isn't it?' He grinned. 'Come on, Nicole. Last night was unfortunate, but I said I'd make it up to you.'

'This isn't about last night!' How dared he try and talk down to her, as if she were just having some kind of illogical PMT moment? 'Look, Luke, I don't want us to fall out. I want us to remain friends—'

'Good, that's what I want too,' he said calmly. 'So, let's clear the air, and then we can get things back to how they were.'

She bit down on her lip. How could she tell him that the problem was that she didn't *want* to get things back to how they were? She didn't want marriage—she'd had that, and it hadn't worked. But she wanted more from a relationship than he was willing to give. She wanted to be with him in every sense. She wanted to be able to go to parties on his arm, she wanted to spend whole nights with him, whole weekends, whole weeks. In short, she wanted to be more than just a bit of fun…she wanted his love.

'Luke, just take my word for it. It is better for us both if we finish it now,' she insisted. 'Otherwise things could get complicated.'

'I don't see how.' He sounded puzzled. 'We've got the perfect agreement…no complications and we both know where we stand. Where's the problem?'

The coolly impassive question made her blood thunder through her veins. How could someone who was so passionate be so damn detached when it came to real feelings?

Thank heaven she hadn't voiced her real reason for finishing things. He'd have looked at her as if she were mad! And maybe she was. Only a mad person would have fallen in love with a man who had clearly told her up-front that he wasn't cut out for relationships. Well, maybe she should end the affair in terms that he would understand.

'Let me just remind you, Luke, that the terms of our agreement were that we had a no-strings affair…just sex.'

'Yes…?' His eyes narrowed on her.

'Well, we've done that—and now I want to move on.' Nicole surprised herself with the level of brisk certainty in her tone. 'So I think you'll find that *you're* the one going against our agreement by subjecting me to this post-mortem.'

'Don't be ridiculous, Nicole!'

'Oh, I'm sorry. Did you think that the rules of our affair were just there to suit *you*?' Her voice shimmered with sarcasm. 'I thought it was a mutual agreement! Silly me!'

'I'm just asking you what the problem is, that's all.' He grated the words harshly. The phone rang on his desk, but instead of picking it up he leaned across and pressed the intercom to speak to his PA. 'Hold all my calls, Sandy,' he snapped impatiently. Immediately the phone stopped ringing.

Nicole noticed that he could ignore his calls when it suited him. The fact added to her annoyance. She also noticed that his cool, laid-back manner had evaporated. Well, good, she thought heatedly. Maybe she was striking a blow for all those women he had dumped in the past without a backward glance. Luke Santana was far too arrogant and blasé for his own good, and it was about time that someone turned the tables on him and let him know that he couldn't have everything his own way.

With that in mind, she moved to pick up her briefcase.

'Where are you going?' he asked with a frown as he watched her.

'It may have escaped your memory, but we have a board meeting to attend,' she said calmly.

'Of course it hasn't escaped my memory!' He glared at her. 'But that can wait for a minute.'

She glanced round at him with a raised eyebrow. 'I don't think so, Luke. Work comes first…remember?'

With a smile she turned and left the room. But as soon as she stepped from the outer office into the lift her mask of cool bravado started to falter. She couldn't believe that she had finished with him—let alone the fact that she had done it so coldly!

For the last few months she had been on such an incredible high…and it had all been due to him. He'd made her feel amazing; he'd made her glow inside with a feeling of exhilaration. She'd had something to look forward to…something to cherish…and now it was over! What the hell had she done?

With difficulty she swallowed down her emotions and told herself that she had done exactly the right thing.

The lift doors opened and she walked out and into the boardroom. It was teeming with people and buzzing with conversation. Most of the directors were already present, but nobody had taken their seats yet. One of the accountants approached her as she went towards her place at the table.

'Ah, Nicole, I wanted to ask you about RJ's sales in the European market...'

She forced herself to concentrate, and strangely the mundane talk about work was soothing...it helped. Slowly her heart-rate was returning to normal. That was until she glanced over and saw that Luke was now in the room. Thankfully he had his back to her, and was talking to one of the directors.

Some people started to take their seats. Molly was refilling the coffeepots at the end of the room. She was going to take minutes for the meeting today. It's just another day, Nicole told herself calmly. A board meeting like millions of others before. Forget about Luke Santana.

He was taking his seat at the top of the table now. Nicole glanced over at him and felt her heart going into overdrive. Hastily she took her papers out and mentally tried to prepare herself.

'When we are all ready...I think we should begin.' His impatient tones cut across the trivial conversation and everyone rushed to take their seats.

And then it was time for Nicole to continue where she had left off yesterday, giving a complete rundown of the RJ Records company and plans for its development once the sale was complete.

Luke watched as she got to her feet. She sounded confident and she looked very together. He couldn't believe that she had just finished things between them. They had been getting on so well…he had really enjoyed making love to her. Just thinking about it now made him lose track of what she was saying, and his eyes drifted over the curves of her body. He liked the way she always dressed in a kind of prim and proper way that somehow managed to make her look even sexier.

Why the hell had she finished things? he wondered again angrily. What was all that nonsense about it being time to move on? He tapped his pen against the papers in front of him and tried to ignore the fact that he'd said similar things to women in the past. This was different… His relationship with Nicole was still red-hot… She knew it…he knew it. So why finish it now?

With difficulty he tried to transfer his mind away from that and back to business. He'd never let a relationship with a woman affect his work, and he wasn't going to start now. He'd just move on, as she suggested. There were other women…

She darted a glance over at him and for a second their eyes met. She had beautiful eyes. Smouldering green, thickly fringed with dark sooty lashes. He didn't want another woman, he realised angrily; he wanted her back in his bed.

Was Nicole seeing someone else? The question flashed into Luke's mind from out of nowhere. It was a possibility. What about the tie that he'd found in her kitchen? She'd told him it was for someone's birthday. At the time he hadn't thought anything about it. But now…

An angry feeling of betrayal seared through him. Then,

annoyed with himself, he shrugged it off. It wasn't like him to think like this. Maybe Nicole was right and it *was* time to move on. Let's face it, he rarely let an affair get past the six-month mark, because he found after that things started to get too heavy. Maybe that was what Nicole was worried about? They had been seeing each other for at least five months now.

But it was a turnaround that *she* had been the one to mention it first. And he didn't like it.

CHAPTER FOUR

WHAT a difference a day made, Nicole thought as she packed her things away ready to leave the office.

This time yesterday all she had been able to think about was getting into bed with Luke and the wild and wonderful effect he had on her. And she had known for sure when their eyes had met that he was thinking along the same lines. Today the relationship was over, and on the few occasions they'd had to speak to each other all hint of warmth and teasing passion had gone from Luke's expression; everything had been completely focused on work.

But what did she expect? she asked herself angrily. Luke wouldn't agonise over their split. In the few seconds he had taken to follow her downstairs into the boardroom this morning he'd probably already lined up another date for tonight.

The thought made her feel desolate.

'Get a grip, Nicole,' she muttered as she headed out towards the lifts.

Molly's desk was empty, as was every office she passed on the way down the hall. It was Friday, and with the urgent work of the week finished most people had gone home about an hour ago. Nicole could have left earlier if she had wanted to, but the thought of her empty apartment and an even emptier weekend stretching before her had not encouraged her to go. It had seemed favourable to bury herself in some paperwork for a while and try to forget it was Friday.

She pressed the button for the lift and then stepped back to wait for it. The only sounds in the building were from the cleaners, who started work when the place was empty. There was the distant hum of vacuum cleaners, a low murmur of voices, and the sound of a radio playing some sentimental love ballad.

Nicole wanted to listen to a love ballad like she wanted a hole in the head. She was about to press the button for the lift again when it suddenly arrived. The doors swished open and to her consternation she was face to face with Luke.

'Oh!' She hesitated. 'I didn't expect to see you. You're working late.'

'That seems to make two of us.' His gaze flicked over her coolly. 'I thought you were going out tonight?'

After a brief hesitation she shrugged. 'I cancelled.'

'I see. Are you getting into the lift or not?'

'Yes, of course.' Hurriedly she stepped in beside him and reached to press the button for the ground floor car park.

There was a moment's silence as the lift doors shut. Nicole was very aware of Luke's eyes on her, and she had never felt more uncomfortable in her life. She searched for something to say to fill the void. 'I've just been filling in that report on the European sales issue.'

Luke made no reply.

'I think we need—'

'Nicole, this is ridiculous!' He cut across her suddenly, his voice calm.

'What is?' Nicole glanced over at him, and as their eyes connected she could feel herself starting to heat up inside.

'You know very well what I mean,' he said gruffly. 'Look, I've thought about what you said this morning and you are right. We shouldn't make heavy weather out of our relationship. But, even so, it seems strange that you are rambling on about European sales and all the while there is an atmosphere between us that needs sorting out.'

'I think we should just concentrate on our work now, Luke.' She looked away from him determinedly. 'I don't really have time for anything else.' She didn't want to get drawn into this conversation. It was an emotional minefield.

'It's six forty-five on a Friday evening, Nicole. I think work can safely take a back seat.'

'On the contrary, I don't think we can afford to be complacent until this deal for RJ is signed.'

His eyes narrowed. 'I'll tell you when we need to concentrate on the deal,' he grated. 'And it's not now. There's no need for you to do any more work on that this evening.'

'Everything has to fit to your requirements, doesn't it, Luke?' She glared at him.

'Well, we managed to fit everything in before,' he said coolly. 'Work and pleasure slotted in together very well, in fact. So what's changed?'

When she didn't answer him immediately, he reached across and to her dismay hit the stop button, causing the lift to grind to a halt between floors.

'What are you doing?'

'We need to talk about what's happened between us.'

'We've said all there is to say.'

'On the contrary, you haven't said nearly enough.' Luke took a step closer. 'I think you owe me a proper explanation,' he said tersely. 'I don't buy all that stuff about work.'

Her heart started to thump against her chest with such violence that it felt like a sledgehammer. 'I don't owe you anything…' She trailed off as he came even closer. 'Luke, I demand that you restart this lift immediately.'

'You demand?' She could see a flicker of amusement in his dark eyes now.

'Yes. I want out of here right now.' She raised her chin defiantly.

'Well, then, the faster you talk, the faster we'll be out of here.'

'There is nothing to talk about,' she said firmly. 'We had an agreement; it was a casual, light-hearted affair. And now it's over. End of discussion.'

He put one hand on the wall at the side of her head and fixed her with a piercingly intense look. 'We were both enjoying ourselves. So why have you finished it?'

'I told you this morning.' It was hard to keep her voice steady and cool. He was too close to her. 'I feel the affair has run its course and—'

'Don't give me all that garbage again, Nicole. I didn't believe it the first time around this morning. I want the real reason.'

'That is the real reason.' Even as she spoke she could feel the sensual awareness twisting between them. He was so close that she could see the gold flecks in his eyes…see the beginning of dark stubble along his jawline. He was so achingly familiar to her. Usually when they were this close she would go into his arms… She longed to do that, to feel his lips pressed close to hers in hungry arousal. 'It's the real reason.' She said the words again, as if by repeating them she could convince herself as well as him.

'So you just woke up this morning and decided suddenly that the affair had run its course?' He sounded scathing.

This was all about his ego, she realised suddenly. He wasn't bothered about losing her…he was bothered because *she* had been the one to finish things. She was probably the first woman who had ever done such a thing, the one that got away, and it was bugging the hell out of him.

'I've been thinking about it for a while, actually.' She raised her chin a little higher and forced herself to hold his gaze. 'Is that so hard to believe?'

'Bearing in mind the steamy passion between us yesterday…quite frankly, yes.'

She tried very hard not to blush…and even harder not to remember what had transpired between them yesterday. 'It was just sex, Luke.'

'No, it wasn't just sex, Nicole.' He said the words with soft emphasis.

'It wasn't?' His words made her heart miss several beats. She felt herself crumble inside as she looked up into his eyes. Had she somehow misread the situation? A ray of hope flared inside her.

'You know it wasn't.' His hand moved to touch her face. The sensations of love and desire that raced through her in that instant were overwhelming.

'So what was it, then?' she asked huskily. She wanted him to say the words…she wanted to hear him say that he cared for her. Even if he couldn't bring himself to mention the L word...a declaration of some emotional intensity would be enough right now. It would be a window of opportunity that would allow her to go back into his arms. And she wanted to do that so badly right now that she ached.

His hand trailed lightly over the side of her face and his eyes were on her lips. 'It was *incredible* sex.'

Nicole felt herself fall from a great height. She flinched away from his hand. Would she never learn? She felt foolish now—foolish to have hoped for even one moment that their relationship had meant anything deeper to him.

Anger burned inside her. 'No, Luke! The real truth is that things were getting stale between us.'

'Really? I hadn't noticed that.' He shrugged. 'There was certainly nothing stale about your responses in the bedroom.'

'Do you have to keep mentioning that?' she asked furiously.

'Well, it *is* relevant,' he said, and looked at her with a raised eyebrow. 'Don't you think?'

'No, I don't. Because the affair is over. And the passion is dead as far as I'm concerned.'

'So the spark between us...whatever it was...has gone?' He clicked his fingers. 'As fast as that?'

'Yes.' She held his gaze defiantly as she tried to convince herself of the fact. 'Now, will you please just restart the lift?'

He ignored her request completely. 'So, if I were to caress you it would have no effect?' he asked quietly.

Her heart missed a beat. 'Luke, I want you to restart the lift!'

A mocking smile played at the corners of Luke's mouth now. 'And if I were to kiss you, you wouldn't want to return the kiss?'

He noticed how her breathing had quickened, how her green eyes had taken on a shimmer of vulnerability.

'Luke—'

He held up his hand. 'Yes, I know—you want out of here.'

She watched with a feeling of relief as he moved back from her and pressed a button, making the lift flare into life.

'So, now we've cleared that up, it's business as usual, then.' He said the words briskly as he looked across at her. 'We'll just forget our little recreational interlude.'

'It's already forgotten.' She tried to sound unconcerned and blasé, but inside she was dying.

The doors opened onto the car park and Nicole wanted to run through them, but she forced herself to walk with dignity past Luke.

'Just one thing.'

His voice made her swing around to look at him, and that was when he caught hold of her and pulled her close against his body.

'I think one last kiss is in order…just to prove to each other that we are doing the right thing.'

'Luke, I—'

Whatever she had been going to say was cut off by the touch of his lips against hers. To her surprise, the kiss wasn't hard or punishing, as the tone of his voice had suggested. On the contrary, it was a gentle assault on her senses. She tried very hard not to respond, her hands stiff by her sides as she willed herself fiercely not to touch him. But the warmth of his caress was so persuasive…so tender…that it made her defences instantly start to collapse. She felt her body starting to weaken, felt her lips starting to soften invitingly as she kissed him back.

It was only as her hands touched against the material of his jacket that she realised she had moved closer. Hurriedly she wrenched herself away. Her breathing was coming in short, sharp bursts; her eyes were wide as they locked on his.

'That wasn't bad, considering the spark has all gone.' Luke's voice was sardonic.

She swallowed hard on a feeling of sadness mixed with fury. 'You shouldn't have done that!' Her voice was trembling now. 'The affair is over, Luke.'

'Of course it is.' He shrugged. 'Relax, there are no hard feelings, Nicole. As you say, the affair would have ground to a halt soon anyway. It was just a bit of fun.'

She folded her arms in front of her body. This didn't feel like fun. This really hurt. But she took another step back from him and just nodded. He was right. If she hadn't finished it, a few weeks down the line he'd have done the deed. At least this way she still had her pride.

The only trouble was that pride seemed a hollow comfort.

'I'll see you next week.' His eyes flicked over her with a look almost of dismissal.

'Yes.' For a second she watched as he headed off towards where his silver Porsche was parked. She was filled with a desire to call out to him, to tell him she had changed her mind and ask could they start over? Hurriedly she fished in her bag for her car keys. She had to remain strong.

Luke was surprised to find that he was filled with anger as he got into his car. It sizzled through him in furious waves. He turned the key in the ignition and the powerful car flared into life. Forget her, he told himself heatedly. She's not worth it. But, even so, anger still pounded through his veins.

No woman had ever acted like this around him before! Maybe that was why he was so incensed, he thought grimly as he swung the car out of his private space and up the ramp into the blinding light of the sun. Maybe she had just dented his ego. Generally *he* was the one who decided when a relationship was over. In fact the last woman to have walked out on him was his mother, and that had been twenty-five years ago, when he was eleven!

He had only driven a block when his phone rang. Pulling over to the side of the road, he reached to answer it.

'Hi, it's me.' Amber Harris's tone was seductively warm.

'Hi, Amber. What can I do for you?'

'I was wondering if you'd like to meet up for a drink tonight?'

The invitation took Luke by surprise, and he didn't answer for a moment.

'You're probably busy, but I just thought I'd ask,' she continued hurriedly.

'Yes, I am busy, Amber.' He found himself fobbing her off. 'I can't make it.'

'Maybe another time?' She sounded disappointed.

'Yes, maybe. Was there anything else, Amber?' Luke continued swiftly.

He listened as she quickly rallied herself and changed the subject back to work.

Why had he turned her down? Luke wondered. Amber was very attractive, and would probably make pleasant company. Not only was he free, he had already made dinner reservations for La Luna tonight—dinner reservations that he had hoped to share with Nicole.

He frowned. Usually he had no qualms about moving

on from a relationship, but strangely the thought of dining with someone else—even someone as attractive as Amber—wasn't firing him with any enthusiasm whatsoever.

Even as Amber was speaking in his mind he was seeing Nicole, and the way she had looked at him a few minutes ago.

Her response to his kiss had held none of its usual dynamism. It had, however, held a curious bittersweet resistance. And that had fired something else inside him… what, he wasn't quite sure. Maybe it was just a sense of challenge?

Whatever it was, he really should just let her go. Should take up Amber's invitation. Trouble was, he didn't want to. He cut across Amber's rambling descriptions of the New York office.

'Look, Amber, I'm going to have to go,' he said impatiently.

'Sure…' She sounded flustered. 'We'll talk later.'

'Yes, I'll look at those last few documents next week.' He closed the phone.

He wasn't ready to move on and date someone else, he thought decisively. What he wanted was Nicole back.

CHAPTER FIVE

THEY were skirting around each other at work, and it had made for an uncomfortable week.

This was what happened when you had an affair with the boss, Nicole thought as she pulled into her parking space at the office with a feeling of dread. Nothing but turmoil ensued.

It certainly felt as if nothing had been going right recently. Not only had she spent the last week trying to convince herself that she was better off without Luke, failing miserably into the bargain, but now she had a particularly nasty bout of food poisoning. She'd been sick all weekend, and it had left her feeling tired and drained. Quite honestly she'd rather have faced the dentist then go and face Luke again for another week of cool, clipped conversations.

And now a third problem was looming. The carefully thought-out business plans for the RJ takeover were in a state of disarray. The owner of the company, Ron Johnson, had failed to sign the contract last Friday.

Nicole had always known that Ron Johnson was unpredictable. He'd built up his business empire with the help of his wife Helen, and since her death just over a year ago he'd been living life as a recluse in the Caribbean, leaving a team of lawyers to organise the sale of his company and becoming more and more intransigent about the terms and conditions under which he would allow his beloved business to leave his possession.

From the outset this deal had been beset with difficulties. Ron's lawyers had wanted to sell to Luke, as his was the highest bid on the table. But Ron had been undecided. He'd had another offer, from a husband and wife team whom he liked, and as he was a deeply religious man he'd said he'd rather sell to them, because he thought they would be more trustworthy and reliable in the workplace.

Nicole found herself remembering the morning a few months ago when Luke had received that news. Their affair had been in full flight, and they'd been working on the first pieces of the jigsaw that would bring RJ Records under their umbrella.

When the phone had rung, and it had been Ron's lawyers *for the fifth time in an hour*, Nicole had had a feeling that more trouble was on its way. They'd already reassured Ron on every aspect of their intentions for the business, but when Luke had heard the latest he'd almost exploded.

'Is the guy *serious*?' he had grated.

'What's the problem?' Nicole remembered she had sat on the edge of his desk and leaned closer.

Luke had flicked on the speakerphone so that she could hear.

'I'm afraid I am serious, Mr Santana. Mr Johnson has deeply held beliefs, and he's also very sentimental about his business. He thinks that a husband and wife team will be the winning combination to look after his company.'

'Well, tell him that *I* run my company with the help of my very trustworthy fiancée,' Luke said sarcastically. 'Tell him anything… In fact tell him we have big plans to turn RJ Records into a family-run business one day.'

'Oh, really?' The lawyer's voice brightened considerably; and the fact that Luke was being completely facetious seemed lost on him. Either that or he had latched on to the statement as a lifeline to push the deal through. 'Well, that might make all the difference, Mr Santana, because I know one of Mr Johnson's concerns is that you might tear the company apart as soon as you acquire it, and sell it off again.'

Luke was struck speechless for a moment.

'I'll tell Mr Johnson about your plans and get back to you,' the lawyer continued briskly. 'I presume the woman in question is the one we have been dealing with? A Ms Connell?'

The lawyer was leading him! Luke glanced over at Nicole with a raised eyebrow. 'Yes, that's the one.'

'Hey! Don't you think you should have asked before using me as your bogus fiancée?' she blazed as soon as the phone call ended.

Luke looked lazily amused. 'It was what you might call a whirlwind decision.'

'Yes, so I noticed—'

'Stop being difficult.' Before she realised his intention he had pulled her down onto his knee and planted a firm yet possessive kiss on her lips. 'It's not a binding commitment…just a temporary stop-gap to please an eccentric millionaire.'

'Hmm…temporary insanity, you mean,' she murmured, distracted by his kiss.

'Well, I can't argue with that... Can you believe that Ron Johnson ever managed to build a business as successful as RJ? Imagine throwing away a deal as big as the one we've offered on some kind of whim! Even his lawyers seem fed-up. That one more or less steered me into a lie!'

'Well, I admire Mr Johnson,' Nicole said staunchly. 'It's not very often that you meet someone who puts ethics above money.'

Luke slanted her a wry look. 'This is just a business deal, Nicole.'

'But it's not just a business deal where Ron Johnson is concerned, is it?' Nicole said. 'He really cares about his company. He and his late wife put a lot of energy into building it up. He wants to sell it to someone with the same moral codes as himself. And he thinks that if he sells it to a husband and wife team it will have a secure future. Whereas if he sells it to you he thinks it could be divided and sold off in little pieces and his workforce could lose their jobs. And, let's face it, he has a point,' Nicole added wryly. 'Because, rather than a warm, family type of man, *you* are an asset-stripping, cold-blooded shark of a businessman.'

Luke shot her an amused look. 'Can I just remind you that this is your fiancé that you are tearing apart?'

'Just thinking laterally,' she said with a smile.

'Well, don't!' He stroked a very sensual caress along the side of her face. 'I'll have you know that I expect loyalty at all times—even from a fake fiancée.'

'Sorry, but I don't know if I can manage that,' she said teasingly.

'Not even with a little persuasion?' He kissed her with a possessiveness that made her heart race.

'Well…on second thoughts I might be open to a little more bribery…' She returned his kisses and wound her arms around his neck.

'So, I wonder if our deal with Johnson is on or off,' Luke said, when they both came up for air.

She smiled and reached up to trail her fingers through his hair. 'Well, put it this way. I hope for your sake that Ron Johnson doesn't read the papers in that remote hideaway of his.'

'Why's that?'

'Because the newspapers refer to you as "The Bachelor Businessman".'

Luke looked amused. 'You are making this up, now.'

'No, it's official: you are a real bad boy. Not only do you break women's hearts, but you also break up companies.'

'It's called asset-stripping, and it is a perfectly legitimate practice.' Luke laughed. 'And as for breaking women's hearts, I think that is a bit of an exaggeration. I'm just not the settling down, pipe-and-slippers type. But I'm always honest and up-front about my intentions.'

'Well, don't shoot the messenger. I'm just telling you what some of the papers say.' Nicole shrugged.

'What kind of newspapers do you read?'

'Quality ones, of course.' Nicole grinned.

'Sounds like it,' Luke said derisively. 'So, the question is: what's a nice girl like you doing with a guy like me?'

'Guess you just got lucky.' She looked at him teasingly. 'Plus, I have to admit I've always been attracted by the element of danger…'

'Ah…now you are talking my language. We seem to have a lot in common, Ms Connell. We both like to take risks.' He stroked a hand along her cheek. 'And we are both free spirits. In fact, I think you are right— I *have* just got lucky. Because you make a great make-believe fiancée.'

It was just a light-hearted remark, but as their eyes connected Nicole felt a brief shimmer of something deeper inside her…a feeling that she immediately dismissed.

Five minutes later they were interrupted by a phone call to tell them that Ron Johnson was willing to go ahead with the deal.

'Thankfully it would appear that Ron reads the financial papers rather than the rags,' Luke said triumphantly as he put the phone down. 'He went for the engagement story.'

'You have no shame, Luke Santana,' she said with a shake of her head. 'Lying without compunction to the poor man.'

'Well, if we are going to be precise, here, it was actually his lawyers who did the lying. And anyway, he's not so poor—he *is* going to get the top price for his business.'

'But he's already a multimillionaire, so maybe the money isn't his real priority.'

'No matter how much money you have, it's still a priority,' Luke said dryly. 'And anyway, haven't you heard that old saying? All's fair in love and business,' he replied with a smile.

'I think you'll find that's love and war,' she corrected. 'There's no mention of *business* in that saying.'

'There is in my book,' Luke said mockingly.

'Well, I think this is a dangerous game,' Nicole warned. 'If Ron finds out that you are lying he will have no choice but to pull the plug on the deal.'

'That is a chance I'll have to take…' He pulled her close with a playful show of strength. 'Now, shall we do something *really* dangerous?' he growled against her ear. 'I feel like celebrating…right here and now…'

Someone was tapping on her car window, and hastily Nicole snapped out of her reminiscences and looked around.

Amber Harris had pulled into the space beside her and come over to attract her attention.

'Oh, hi, Amber.' Hurriedly Nicole reached for her briefcase and stepped out to join her.

'You looked like you were miles away,' the other woman remarked cheerfully as they walked together towards the lifts.

'I was just thinking about all the work I've got lined up for today,' Nicole said briskly. 'I've got a load of new contracts to sort out.'

'Tell me about it!' Amber tossed her mane of long red hair over one shoulder as they stepped into the lift. She was wearing a tight little black dress, and it looked fabulous on her. She was more like a top model than an accountant, Nicole thought wryly.

'I'm sorting out figures for the New York office,' Amber said. 'I had to fly there three times last week. I've got to the point where I don't know what city I'm in.'

'That can be very tiring,' Nicole said sympathetically.

'You are not kidding!' Amber pressed the button for the top floor. 'The only thing that keeps me going is Luke. He is just so gorgeous, isn't he?' She leaned back against the wall of the lift and sighed dreamily.

'Yes, very good-looking.' Nicole pressed the button for her floor.

'He's a hard fish to catch, though. I know lots of women have tried to pin him down and failed. But that makes him all the more of a challenge, don't you think?'

'I suppose so.' Had *she* seen Luke as a challenge? Nicole thought about that for a moment and then dismissed it. No, she had originally seen Luke as exciting and fun. She had never set out to want more than that. In fact after her divorce the last thing she had wanted was to fall in love again, and she had thought that being with Luke would be playing things safe emotionally. It was a damn disaster. Life would have been so much easier if she could have just continued enjoying their affair for what it was.

'Anyway, I think he might be on the verge of asking me out to dinner next week.' Amber looked over at her conspiratorially. 'Well, put it this way…I'm working on it.'

Somehow Nicole managed a smile. She was used to women swooning over Luke. And it was none of her business if he chose to go out with someone else now. But even so she couldn't quite get rid of a swirling feeling of loss. *Stop it, Nicole*, she told herself fiercely. *You have to let go of him.*

At least nobody knew about the affair, she consoled herself. Things would be far worse if she were now the subject of office gossip. Swiftly she changed the subject. 'I'm up to my eyes in this RJ Records deal.'

'I heard there are problems with that, and Ron Johnson hasn't signed the contract.'

'Just a blip,' Nicole said with confidence. 'We've had these before with him.'

'Aaron Williams thinks the deal will fold.'

Privately, Nicole was having similar doubts—but she wasn't going to voice them aloud. As long as there was a spark of life left in this deal she was going to fight for it. 'We'll get the company,' she said determinedly. 'It's just a matter of time.' The lift opened on Nicole's floor. 'See you later, Amber.'

Would Luke go out with Amber? Nicole wondered as she walked down towards her office. Every time she thought about it she felt a dart of some dark and horrible emotion twisting inside her.

With determination she turned her attention back towards work. The important thing was finalising this deal with Johnson.

As soon as Nicole sat down at her desk she checked her e-mails. There was nothing regarding the RJ deal. The silence was ominous.

She supposed she would have to check with Luke to find out how he wanted to play things.

Nicole was just reaching for the phone so that she could ring and discuss it with him when an e-mail arrived from him.

You better come up so we can sort this RJ mess out.

No *Good morning, Nicole, how are you?* she thought sardonically as she ran a smoothing hand over her hair and tried to prepare herself for facing him. She could have done without this, she thought as she got reluctantly to her feet. She still felt a bit nauseous; obviously that food poisoning bug hadn't completely gone.

When she walked into Luke's office she found that she wasn't the only one to have been summoned. His lawyer, Aaron Williams, was there, and so was the company's chief accountant, John Sorenson. Luke was pacing around the room like a caged lion.

How was it that Luke could even look sexy when he was

angry? Nicole wondered hazily. He seemed to radiate some kind of forceful energy that was compelling. Maybe it was something as simple as the fact that he looked good in that dark suit. Or maybe it was that attitude of power and dynamism… She didn't know. All she knew was that life would be a lot easier if she were immune to him.

'What took you so long, Nicole?' he asked tersely. 'I've had Ron's lawyers on the phone…' Luke trailed off and looked at her again, his eyes narrowed. 'Are you OK? You look a bit pale.'

'I'm fine,' she lied, surprised he'd noticed.

He looked at her intently for a second, and her heart seemed to skip a beat. *Don't start imagining he gives a damn, for heaven's sake,* she reminded herself fiercely. She angled up her chin a little further. 'I'm fine, Luke,' she reiterated firmly.

He nodded. 'Well, we've got a busy few days ahead of us, so I hope so. This is a crucial time for the business.'

There… All he was worried about was the fact that she might need time off work, and she'd been wondering if he was concerned about her, Nicole thought angrily.

'Anyway, getting back to the matter in hand,' Luke continued speedily, 'the bottom line is that Ron wants to meet with me before he signs the contact.'

'So he *is* going to sign?' Nicole sank down into one of the office chairs.

Luke shrugged. 'Your guess is as good as mine. But we've come this far down the road, so we'll have to go with whatever he wants right now.'

'I've gone over the figures with a fine comb and I think he would be mad not to sign,' John put in heatedly. He was pouring some coffee from a pot that was standing on the desk. 'Do you want a drink, Nicole?'

She shook her head. The mere thought of drinking coffee was making her stomach clench in protest.

With difficulty, she tuned back in to what Luke was saying.

'I don't think it's the money that's the problem. Apparently he wants other assurances, otherwise he's backing out.'

'What kind of assurances?' Nicole asked cautiously. *Was this anything to do with Luke's lie about being engaged?* she wondered suddenly.

'Heaven knows what it is this time,' Luke grated. 'But we are going to have to meet with him today—before the whole deal collapses.'

'Today?' Nicole was taken aback. 'That's too short notice!'

Luke was distracted as she crossed her long shapely legs and sent him a very feisty look from fulminating green eyes. 'It's going to have to be today,' he muttered. 'Talking through lawyers isn't helping. And if we let this drag on any longer we are going to lose the deal.'

'But Ron is virtually a recluse.' She frowned. 'And he lives in a remote hideaway on Barbados, Luke. He won't come here.'

'Yes, I realise that,' Luke said dryly. 'Which is why I've put the company jet on standby.' He glanced at his watch. 'I reckon if we get our act together we can be on the plane and heading off within the hour.'

Nicole started to shake her head. She didn't like the sound of this at all. 'Ron is eccentric, Luke. You know we could go all that way and he might change his mind about seeing us.'

'I don't think that will happen. He said he wants to meet, and he sounded genuine,' Luke said firmly.

'But we'd need a copy of all the paperwork.' Her heart was thumping very uncomfortably now, and it had nothing to do with paperwork and everything to do with the thought of going away on business with Luke. 'And—'

'And Aaron is going to take care of all that.' Luke cut across her swiftly and turned to look at the other man, who was standing silently by the window. 'I'll need it on my desk within half an hour.'

Aaron looked shocked. 'It might take a bit longer—'

'We haven't got longer than that.' Luke cut across him too. 'So I suggest you get a move on.'

'Fine.' Aaron departed from the room, looking immensely agitated.

'And meanwhile I want you to check the figures, John.' Luke turned towards his chief accountant. 'Print out some variations on the theme, in case we have to renegotiate the price.'

'Yes, I'll get right on it.' John swept out of the room, looking as flustered as Aaron.

Nicole couldn't blame them. It wasn't easy to be around Luke when he was in one of these moods. He was a perfectionist, and he didn't tolerate setbacks easily.

There was a tense silence when they were left alone.

'So, what would you like me to do?' Nicole asked hesitantly.

'You better go home and pack enough clothes for a few days.'

'A few *days*!' Nicole looked over at him in surprise. 'This should be an overnight trip at most!'

'I don't know how long it's going to take to sort out. But

we'll have to stay there until we have some kind of handle on it.' Luke perched on the edge of his desk and looked over at her. And despite the seriousness of the situation he couldn't help but feel a certain sense of satisfaction from the words. Maybe at the same time he could get some kind of a handle on Nicole's innermost emotions, he thought suddenly…find out what she was thinking… He'd tolerated this cool, clipped politeness of hers for a week now, and it was driving him insane.

He smiled to himself. 'And *you* are going to have to play the part of my fiancée.'

Nicole felt her face flare with colour. 'Are you joking?'

'No.' Luke's voice was calm. 'This isn't really a joking matter, is it?'

'I told you that you were playing with fire when you lied to Ron!' She glared at him. 'Is this why the deal has stalled? Does he know you fed him a load of rubbish?'

'I've no idea, Nicole,' he said honestly. 'All I'm saying is I am going to need you by my side to play your part. Hopefully it won't take long.'

'I'm not happy about this approach to things, Luke,' she said in agitation. 'I think it's most unprofessional.'

'I'm not wild about it myself, but what can we do?' He shrugged. 'I need you to come with me regardless of the fiancée angle. You've done most of the negotiations. You know this deal backwards.'

He was right. This deal was her baby; she'd nursed it for months. There was no way she was going to cut herself out from it now. 'I'll get Molly to book some accommodation for us, then,' she said decisively.

'No need. I've got a house out there. Accommodation

is the least of our worries.' Luke glanced over as she continued to sit there. 'Is there a problem?'

'Well…' She shrugged. The problem was that this was giving her palpitations! The fact that they would be staying at his house rather than at a hotel seemed to make everything worse. She tried to make herself feel better with the thought that Aaron and John would be accompanying them. But, even so, it seemed much too intimate a situation, given their present circumstances.

'Nicole?' He was watching her with a frown.

Quickly, she rallied. 'I'm finding it hard to get my head around this lie you've told to Ron Johnson, but I don't suppose there is a lot we can do about that now.' She didn't know what else she could say. Telling him she didn't want to stay at his house would sound as if she didn't trust herself when she was around him…which to be honest she didn't. But she couldn't let him know that! She was just going to have to be very strict with herself and dedicate her every thought towards the deal and not him. 'We'll just have to deal with the situation, I suppose. This is too important for us to muck it up now.'

'My sentiments exactly. So at least we understand each other.' His voice was filled with cool authority. 'I'll pick you up outside your apartment in half an hour. Make sure you have all the relevant paperwork with you.'

Nicole stood up and, with a nod, made for the door.

Luke watched her go with a gleam of satisfaction.

Maybe this could all work to his advantage. With Nicole by his side Ron might sign the contract, and at the same time Nicole would be forced closer to him… Which meant he could get past those prickly defences of hers and find out the real reason why she had pushed him away…and in the process maybe he'd get lucky, both in business and in bed.

The thought put a positive spin on the day.

CHAPTER SIX

THERE was no time for Nicole to dwell on the situation. By the time she had driven back to her apartment and thrown things into a case the buzzer was ringing and Luke was telling her impatiently through the intercom that he was waiting downstairs.

She glanced at her reflection in the full-length mirror before picking up her small suitcase. There hadn't been time to change, so she was still wearing the pale blue suit she had been wearing at the office this morning. At least there was colour in her cheeks now—probably due more to agitation than perfect health, But at any rate she no longer looked like death warmed up, so that was something.

The buzzer rang again. 'Yes, I'm coming,' she muttered angrily as she struggled through the door and into the lift with her briefcase and her suitcase.

She hadn't expected Luke to be outside in a limousine! A chauffeur jumped out of the vehicle as she appeared, and took her suitcase before opening the door for her.

She sank down into the comfortable leather seat opposite Luke. 'Sorry to keep you waiting,' she said breathlessly.

'That's OK.' By contrast, Luke appeared to be perfectly

relaxed. He had some paperwork open in front of him and he barely glanced up at her. 'But we *are* cutting things fine.'

'I had to pack and…' She trailed off as she suddenly noticed that they were alone. 'Where's Aaron and John? I thought they were coming with us?'

She had his full attention now. 'What gave you that idea?'

'I don't know…I just assumed…' She took a deep breath and forced herself to sound calm. She didn't want him to realise she was shaken by the fact they were alone. 'I mean, don't we need them? Aaron's legal advice could be crucial. I usually have a team with me when I go on these business trips. Last year when I went to LA I took—'

'Nicole.' Luke looked straight at her, his eyes steely. 'I'm the president of the company. I make the decisions. You don't need anyone else with you.'

She clammed up. When he put it like that, she supposed he was right.

'Now, do you think we could get on with some work? I need you to run your eye over these figures that John has produced.'

Nicole took some of the sheets of paper he handed across to her and tried to concentrate.

For a while there was silence between them as the limousine glided smoothly through the traffic. Nicole finished reading the report and then opened her briefcase to get some paper to make notes. Her glance flicked around the vehicle. She had never travelled in this much style before. Her usual run to the airport was made squashed into a cab with others from the office. This vehicle was enormous, and impressively kitted out with a circular sweep of black leather seats, a mini-bar and TV.

'Do you usually travel like this when you go away on business?' she asked impulsively.

He glanced over at her. 'Yes, of course.'

Stupid question, Nicole berated herself. Luke's whole life was one of luxury.

Home for him was a fabulous apartment in the Art Deco district of Miami. It overlooked the beach and had its own rooftop terrace with a swimming pool. Nicole had only been there a few times, and she had thought the place absolutely beautiful. But she hadn't liked it. The decor was smart and trendy, but geared towards the fact that it was a bachelor pad…and a multimillionaire bachelor pad at that. It had every hi-tech modern convenience you could wish for, and it was coldly impersonal.

She supposed she hadn't liked it because it had reminded her of the things she wanted to forget about Luke. Not only that he wasn't one for putting down roots, but also that they lived in two different worlds. Yes, she was successful enough to be able to rent a beautiful apartment in a nice area, but it was nothing compared to Luke's life. He had houses all over the world…chauffeur-driven limousines…a company jet, for heaven's sake!

Even if he *had* been the settling down type, their relationship probably wouldn't have worked out anyway. He'd have chosen someone from his own social sphere.

He looked up suddenly and caught her watching him, and as his dark eyes sliced into hers it set her heart thundering crazily against her chest. It brought home the fact that she could try and persuade herself all day about why their relationship wouldn't have worked out, but she was still in love with him.

'Would you like a drink?' Luke asked suddenly as he reached to pour himself a coffee from a pot beside the bar. 'There is fruit juice and mineral water if you don't want coffee.'

'I'd love a mineral water, please.' She watched as he reached and opened one of the bottles, then poured it into a crystal glass for her.

'Thanks.' She took the drink from him, being careful to avoid touching his hand. Her eyes looked up towards his, and she knew he had noticed the fact because there was a look of irritation in their dark depths.

'We are not going to have this atmosphere between us for the next few days, are we?' he asked suddenly, his tone derisive.

'What atmosphere?' She tried to ignore the fact that her skin was heating up.

'You seem edgy.'

'Look, as far as I'm concerned this is work as usual, OK?' Her eyes clashed with his across the confined space.

Then he nodded. 'Good. That's OK, then.'

The ring of his mobile phone broke the mood, and Nicole turned her gaze back towards her work with a feeling of relief. He was right. If this feeling of tension were kept up for much longer she would be like a wrung-out dishcloth in no time.

'Oh, hi, Amber,' he said lightly. 'I'm just on my way to the airport now. Did you find that report? That's great. Well, if you would, that would make life easier...' He laughed at whatever she said in reply. It was that lazy, attractive laugh that made Nicole's pulses race. With a frown she tried to bury herself further into her paperwork.

'Yes, OK—I'll see you soon,' he said, and laughed again at what she said.

He obviously found Amber extremely amusing. Nicole was filled with a childish urge to put her fingers in her ears. She really didn't want to hear this. See you soon for what? she wondered suddenly. Dinner…*bed*?

'Yeah, I'll look into that. OK, bye.'

He hung up and silence resumed between them. Nicole glared at her work. She was being ridiculous. Amber worked for Luke. OK, she fancied him like crazy, but despite what she had told Nicole in the lift that didn't mean there was something going on between them. And even if there were it wouldn't last. A few months down the line and Luke would be bored, ready for the next conquest. Trouble was, that fact didn't really cheer Nicole up—because just the thought of Luke kissing another woman…taking her to bed…filled her with a feeling of complete and utter desolation. It was wildly irrational, but she couldn't seem to help it.

She had felt like this when her marriage had fallen apart and Patrick had told her he was leaving her. But she'd had more reason to be upset back then. She'd been married to Patrick for five years, and not only had he been leaving her for someone else but the other woman had been pregnant with his child.

She could still remember the gut-wrenching feeling when he'd told her the news.

To find out that Patrick had had an affair was bad enough, but to discover he was also about to become a father was a double-whammy.

She would never forget the moment he had dropped the bombshell. He'd even had the nerve to tell her that he still loved her. 'The affair only started out as a bit of fun,' he had said sadly. 'A bit of light entertainment. I never meant to hurt you. But the thing is that she's going to have my baby…I can't walk away from her now. I've got to do the right thing.'

The right thing! That was a joke. Nicole had told him that if he had wanted to do 'the right thing' he would never have had an affair in the first place.

She had wanted to throw things at him; she had wanted to rail against the world and him for the cruelty and unfairness. Why couldn't it have been *her* baby? But instead she had conducted herself with cool dignity, picked herself up and carried on with her life. And she'd promised herself that no man would ever hurt her again. It was a promise that she was clinging on to for grim life at the moment.

She bit down on her lip and tried to remind herself of the lessons from the past. She had loved Patrick…or rather she had thought she loved him until he had walked out and she had found out he was really very shallow. Even so, her divorce had devastated her. It had been a sobering lesson on guarding her heart, and most of all on the importance of being independent.

So she had been right to finish with Luke. Especially as her feelings for him were even more intense than anything she had felt for Patrick. She couldn't go through any more pain; she didn't need a man in her life, she told herself firmly.

They were thirty-five thousand feet up in the sky and it felt as if they were nearly as many miles apart, Luke thought irately as he spoke to Nicole for the third time and got a one-word reply.

He glanced across at her. He couldn't see her face; it was obscured from view by the silky curtain of her hair. She'd been sitting like that since take-off, deeply immersed in a report he'd handed her. And although he couldn't fault her behaviour—she was businesslike and courteous—there was something really irritating about the way she had completely withdrawn from him. In the old days when they were working together on reports she would give him a smile or say something amusing. She had a great sense of humour and could usually make him laugh no matter how dry the subject they were immersed in. He missed that.

Luke drummed his fingers on the edge of the table. He had a million and one checks to make before this meeting with Ron. He didn't have time for frivolities. And yet…he found his gaze constantly drifting over towards her.

She had taken off the jacket to her blue suit and was wearing a plain white blouse that was neatly tailored into her small waist. He noticed that her pencil skirt stopped just above her knee. She uncrossed her long legs and then crossed them again. His eyes followed the movement. Then he noticed that her pen had rolled down onto the floor. Before he could pick it up for her she had bent to retrieve it. Her blouse was buttoned low and he could just see the edge of her lacy white bra.

He badly wanted to make love to her again, but he knew this was a game he needed to play carefully. One wrong move and like a skittish colt she might bolt in the opposite direction. Over this last week he had forced himself to bide his time and match her businesslike mood. It was strange, patience wasn't usually one of his virtues, but somehow Nicole was worth waiting for.

No matter what she had said to him about how the spark had gone, how she wanted to move on, he didn't quite believe her. OK, maybe he was being arrogant and over-confident…and maybe she was seeing someone else…he hadn't entirely ruled out the possibility. But he had tasted desire on her lips when he had last kissed her. He was almost sure of it. And now they were going to be alone together…the perfect time to find out what was going on…to get inside her head, sort things out and then hopefully enjoy some passion. Except for one small flaw. She was ignoring him.

He raked an impatient hand through his hair, irritated with himself for dwelling on this now. He should think about this tonight, when business was out of the way. This meeting with Johnson had to be given his full attention. *Snooze and you lose*, he told himself firmly.

He got up and walked over towards the refrigerator at the other side of the plane. 'Do you fancy something to eat?' he asked over his shoulder.

'No, thanks.' She didn't look up.

Luke helped himself to a sandwich and poured himself more coffee. 'Would you like a drink?'

'No, thanks.'

Hell, but she was really irritating him now. He sat back in his seat and rustled through some papers.

'You drink too much caffeine,' she said suddenly. 'That's your fourth cup. I'm surprised you can sleep at night.'

So she had been noticing what he was doing even if she wasn't looking up. 'I never have any difficulty sleeping.' He looked over at her and smiled.

She gave a brief shadow of a smile back, and then returned her attention to her report.

'You should really eat something, you know,' he said.

'I'm not hungry.' She glanced over at him and their eyes met.

'Are you OK?' he asked, with a sudden pang of concern. She hadn't looked well earlier, and now that he studied her she still looked a little drawn.

'You asked me that this morning. And I told you I'm fine.'

'You didn't look fine this morning. You looked like death warmed up.'

'Gee, thanks.'

He smiled at her. 'Just trying to show some friendly concern.'

'I think I prefer you in your usual indifferent and domineering mode.'

'Well, as you have put in a request, a little bit of domineering could be arranged…' He looked at her teasingly.

Nicole tried to ignore the fact that when he looked at her like that she felt her temperature rise to boiling point. She hated herself for being so susceptible to him.

'I think we are getting off track, Luke. We should be discussing our forthcoming meeting, not—'

'You know, Nicole, just because our affair is over, it doesn't mean we can't still be friends.' Luke cut across her suddenly, his voice firm.

The words caused Nicole's heart to thump even more fiercely against her chest. Could you ever really go back to being just friends with someone you had shared such incredible passion with? she wondered. Certainly at this moment, feeling the way she did about him, she didn't think that was even remotely possible. How could you ever truly forget that you loved someone?

'Yes, of course we are friends.' She made herself say the words lightly.

'So why do I detect a frosty tone?'

'There is no frosty tone.' She looked over at him and then, as their eyes met, wished she hadn't. 'I'm just dealing with the situation as best I can,' she admitted huskily. 'Obviously it's a bit...awkward to be away on business with someone...you used to be close with.'

'I don't see why it has to be awkward,' Luke said nonchalantly.

'Well, I suppose you wouldn't,' she muttered, annoyed by his casual manner. 'I suppose you are used to jumping from one relationship to another, but I'm not.'

'But this is *your* choice, Nicole,' he grated.

How had they managed to slide onto such dangerous ground? she wondered in sudden panic. 'Yes, and it's fine. We've both moved on and we've been working well together this last week. As far as I'm concerned there's no *real* problem. You brought the subject up, not me.'

'Because I think if we are to have a good working relationship it's important that we are relaxed around each other. I don't think we should let personal issues get in the way of us doing good work.'

That was all he was ever worried about...work. 'I agree wholeheartedly.' She frowned and looked back at the papers in front of her. 'I just want us to get on and get this situation over with. Then we can go our separate ways and *really* relax.'

'There! That's what I mean! There's that frosty tone

again! You're going to have to watch that, Nicole. We'll never convince Ron Johnson that you are my fiancée if you sound like that around him!'

Her head jerked up at that. 'So that's what this is about!' She glared at him. 'You are not so worried about us being friends as pulling a fast one on Ron Johnson!'

'I am not pulling a fast one on anybody,' he said firmly.

'Yes, you are. You've lied, and in my book that's sharp practice!'

'You agreed to go along with the lie, so you are not so innocent yourself,' he grated sardonically.

'Only because I didn't have any choice in the matter!'

'Well, as I remember it, you didn't put up that much of a fight at the time.' His voice was coolly taunting, and it whipped Nicole's already delicate emotions into a fury. 'In fact as I recall we sealed the agreement with a kiss.'

How dared he throw what had been a romantic moment back in her face? 'Let's just drop this conversation, shall we?' she suggested coolly. 'This is exactly why we can't be friends.'

'Why? Because I'm reminding you of the truth?'

'Because you irritate the hell out of me, that's why!' she flared.

Luke smiled. 'That's better.'

'What's better?' She frowned.

'You,' he said firmly. 'You're back to your old self. That "yes and no" polite act was really starting to annoy me. I get that from everyone else around me. I expect more from you.'

'Really?' Her voice was cool. 'Well, I expect more from you than to throw reminders of intimate moments at me.'

'You can be a real spoilsport, Nicole,' he drawled with a laugh.

'And you can be a real pain in the…neck!'

'So I take it my *let's be friends* suggestion is out the window, then?' he said humorously.

'Oh, don't worry. I'll play my part and be the devoted fiancée around Ron,' she muttered. 'But that doesn't mean I'll like it.'

'I'd never have guessed.'

Luke's calm sarcasm did nothing to make her feel better. 'Well, maybe you should have used some other woman as your fake better half.'

'Maybe I should,' Luke agreed with a shrug. 'But it's a bit late for that. And as you are dealing with the RJ takeover, I'll just have to make do with you, won't I?'

The atmosphere wasn't just frosty now, it was downright arctic. Nicole looked away from him. Silence descended again between them.

The man was impossible, Nicole thought angrily. How dared he say he'd just have to *make do* with her? He was arrogant and insufferable.

Thirty minutes later the fasten seatbelt sign came on and the pilot announced that they would soon be landing. She glanced at her watch as Luke packed away some of his papers.

His arm touched against hers when he leaned across to look out of the window, and instantly she felt tingles of awareness shooting through her in a way that sent all her strong thoughts about how she disliked him into disarray. How was it that no matter how tense the situation got between them she *still* wanted to melt when he touched her? How long would it take her to get over feeling like this? she wondered painfully. *Weeks? Months? Maybe years?* a little voice said mockingly.

'Looks like a nice day down there,' he said easily.

'Does it?' Swiftly she turned away from him and glanced out of the window. Below she could see the sparkling blue water of the Caribbean, and then, as the plane banked, the green swathe of an island fringed with palm trees and golden beaches.

'Beautiful, isn't it?' Luke said.

How could he act so cool when they had just had a blazing row? she wondered. It really irritated her that he could just switch off from feelings; he'd done it when they were together as well…made love to her with fierce passion and then ten minutes later switched from lover to businessman. She hated it.

'Yes, it is.' She returned her gaze down towards the report on her knee, but she was still aware that his shoulder was just touching against hers.

Luke drummed his fingers against the armrest between them. She tried not to notice…tried not to think about the way those hands could rouse her to wonderful heights of passion.

'Shall I put this away for you now?' Suddenly Luke reached and took the report away from her. 'You need to prepare yourself for landing and fasten your belt.'

'Yes, I know that, Luke. But it doesn't affect my ability to read,' she said coolly.

'You've done enough reading. We're on Caribbean time now, so we can be a little more laid back.'

'Not if we want to get around this problem with Ron Johnson,' she reminded him as she snapped her seatbelt shut.

There she was, turning the tables on him again! Reminding him of the importance of work! The fact that she was right annoyed him. Usually *he* was the one who was completely focused. What the hell was the matter with him? he wondered.

He watched as she opened her bag and took out a comb to smooth it through her long, sleek hair. Then she opened a compact and checked her make-up, reapplied the frosty amber colour to her lips.

She had very kissable lips...he thought. This was the problem, he decided distractedly. He needed to get her back in his life and in his bed. Then things would return to normal and he could stop feeling on edge and concentrate properly on work again.

'What time is our meeting?' she asked as she snapped the compact closed and put her bag back under her seat.

'Ron's invited us for dinner at six-thirty.' Luke glanced at his watch. 'We'll just have time to get to my place and change first.'

'Dinner?' Nicole's eyebrows lifted. 'Considering the guy is virtually a recluse, that sounds encouraging. You know he doesn't usually see anybody except his lawyers and the manager he put in charge of the company?'

'Yes, he's an eccentric. But I played on the fact that we are virtually neighbours in Barbados, and it gave me an advantage.'

'Great. Well, hopefully we can get things sorted out quickly. Maybe we'll even be able to come straight back tonight.'

'Maybe.' His eyes held with hers steadily. 'But I wouldn't bet on it,' he said firmly.

CHAPTER SEVEN

THERE was a limousine waiting for them outside the terminal. They sat side by side without speaking as it whisked them down narrow country roads lined with sugar cane.

The mood between them was only broken by the fact that Luke had opened the glass partition to talk to their driver, who was an extremely friendly Barbadian called George. He laughed and joked with them, and Nicole started to relax a little as she looked out at the rolling green countryside.

They stopped when they reached the entrance to Luke's house, and waited for huge electric gates to fold back.

'We are expecting a storm tonight,' George said as he put the car into gear again and they swept on, up a long driveway.

Nicole looked up at the clear blue sky through the tracery of palm trees. 'But there's not a cloud in sight.'

'It's heading in, all right. Should be with us in the early hours of tomorrow morning.'

'I hope it's not a hurricane,' Nicole said lightly. 'I experienced a storm in Miami last year, and it was frightening.'

'I think we are lucky. It *was* hurricane force, but its strength is dropping.' George grinned at her. 'But these tropical storms are as unpredictable as a woman, so you never know.'

The car pulled to a halt and Nicole turned her attention to her surroundings. They were outside a most magnificent period house that was steeped in character.

It was painted white, and had wooden shutters that opened out onto a wraparound veranda. Bright swathes of tropical flowers grew up along the balconies, and behind the riot of colour and greenery she could see white wicker furniture, placed to look out over a garden that sloped gently down towards the sea.

Nicole let out her breath in a sigh. 'Wow.' It was all she could say.

Luke slanted an amused look over at her. 'I take it you approve?'

'Who wouldn't approve of this? It's idyllic.'

George opened the door for them and they stepped out of the air-conditioned car into the heat of the day.

There was a lazy tranquillity about the place, a silence that was infinitely soothing. The only noise was the gentle wash of waves against the shore and the occasional drone of a bee amongst the old-fashioned climbing roses.

They walked up into the shade of the veranda as the front door swung open and a woman in her mid-fifties greeted them. Her ample frame was squeezed into a bright floral dress and she had a round, smiling face. There was something warm and friendly about her, and Nicole immediately liked her.

'Welcome home, Mr Santana,' she gushed. 'I have everything ready for you.'

'Thanks, Deloris.' Luke reached and shook the woman by the hand. 'I'd like you to meet my business associate, Nicole Connell,' he said smoothly. 'Deloris is my housekeeper, Nicole, and a fine job she does too. I don't know what I'd do without her.'

The woman beamed with pleasure. 'Anything you need, Ms Connell, don't hesitate to ask me.'

They followed her into the house across a wide hallway with polished wood floors. Nicole glimpsed a very elegant drawing room to her left, before proceeding up the wide curving staircase.

'I've put you in the guest suite, Ms Connell,' Deloris said as she opened a door along the landing with a flourish.

Nicole walked past Luke into a large bedroom with a wooden four-poster bed. French doors were open out onto the veranda, and Nicole could see the bright blue of the Caribbean Sea. 'This is really lovely. Thank you.'

'I'm glad you like it.' Deloris turned towards her employer, who was standing just outside the doorway. 'There have been a few phone calls for you, Mr Santana.'

As Deloris reeled off a seemingly never-ending list of names, Nicole perched herself on the edge of the bed. She felt a little tired… In fact she felt like lying down. It was probably the heat; there didn't seem to be any air-conditioning, just the overhead whirl of the ceiling fans.

Deloris finished with her list of messages and then moved on to ask about requirements for dinner.

'We are going out, thanks, Deloris,' Luke said easily. 'Mr Johnson is sending a boat for us.'

'A boat?' Nicole looked over at him in surprise as the housekeeper left them.

'Yes. Apparently the only way to access Ron's house is by boat. He's a bit manic about security, it seems.'

'Well, if we are travelling by boat, I suppose I better put some flat-heeled shoes on, then.' Nicole kicked off her high heels and rubbed her foot absently.

Her skirt had ridden up a little. Luke followed the line of her body with narrowed eyes. 'Nicole?'

'Yes?' Her hair swung back as she looked over at him, her green eyes wide and questioning.

Luke hesitated. What the hell was he going to say to her? *Don't rub your foot like that...it's turning me on?* It sounded crazy...even to his ears. 'Never mind,' he grated impatiently. 'We haven't got long, so get a move on, will you?'

Then he was gone, closing the door very firmly behind him. Tonight, after they'd sorted out business, he would seduce her back into his bed, he promised himself. And order would be restored in his life.

When Nicole went downstairs twenty minutes later she followed the sound of Luke's voice and found him in a large study with doors that were open onto the garden.

He was sitting behind a desk with his laptop computer open in front of him. 'Bear with me for a moment,' he said, covering the phone as Nicole walked in. 'Nicole, do you remember how we access the files for RJ's accounts?' His eyes flicked over her as she walked closer, taking in the white slim-fitting trousers and the crossover black and white top. She looked smart, and yet sexy at the same time. How did she manage to do that? he wondered absently as he pressed another key to try to get the screen he wanted.

'Here.' She walked behind him and leaned over. He

could smell the scent of her perfume, sultry like a summer's day. 'We hid the files under a code…remember?'

As he watched she keyed in the code, and instantly the right file opened.

'Thanks. I'd forgotten we'd done that.' He picked up the phone again and resumed his conversation. But out of the corner of his eye he was watching Nicole as she walked around the room. She picked up a photograph of his father that was sitting next to the bookshelves. And then admired a watercolour painting that hung over the fireplace.

'This house isn't at all what I expected,' she said idly once he had hung up.

'And what *did* you expect?' Luke asked as he leaned back in his chair.

She was looking at a porcelain figurine now, which was on the windowsill. 'Well, the décor in your apartment in Miami is kind of… I suppose, at the risk of sounding rude, it's clinical…in a very stylish way, of course,' she added hastily.

'Clinical?'

'Yes…you know. Impersonal—as if everything in it isn't really your choice, it's been designed for you.'

'That's because it *was* designed for me,' Luke said with amusement. 'I paid an interior designer. I haven't got time for décor, Nicole. I'm too busy running my businesses.'

'Yes, I know.' She looked over at him. 'But this place is more of a home, somehow.'

'It was my home for a while,' Luke said with a shrug. 'My parents moved here from Portugal when I was nine.'

'I didn't realise!' Nicole looked around again with renewed interest. 'It must have been an idyllic place to grow up.'

'It was OK.' Luke glanced at his watch.

'So where are your parents now?' she asked.

'My father is dead and my mother lives in France.' Luke stood up. 'We better sort out a few last-minute details on this deal and make tracks. We don't want to be late for Ron.'

'No, of course not.'

She noticed how when the conversation veered towards something personal he only gave the briefest information and then quickly moved on. It had always been like that with him. Luke had never talked about his childhood, or shared any secrets from his past with her. And when she thought about it that hurt. They had snuggled up together in bed in the most intimate way and Nicole had longed to talk to him…really talk to him…get to know him on a deeper level. Yet he never had truly opened up to her. Yes, he'd held her after lovemaking, and he had made her feel special. But then, just as she had begun feeling closer to him than to any person in the world, he'd always pulled away…talked about business…talked about practicalities…never emotions…

She watched as he walked over towards one of the cupboards and took out a wooden box. 'What are you doing?'

'You need an engagement ring.' As he spoke he was emptying out the contents of the box on his desk.

Some old costume jewellery spilled across the leather top.

'Where did you get all that?' she asked curiously.

'It belonged to my mother.' He opened some more drawers in the box and searched around before pulling out a velvet case. 'Ah, here we are.' He opened the lid and Nicole could see a square-cut diamond ring glinting in the sunlight.

He took it out, and then to her surprise tossed it casually in her direction. 'Here—try it on for size.'

She only just caught it. 'This looks very expensive,' she said as she looked down at it.

'Well, I think Ron will expect to see a nice ring on your finger.' He nodded towards it. 'Go ahead, try it on.'

With a feeling of extreme trepidation she slipped it on. 'It's a fraction too big.' She was about to take it off again, but before she could Luke walked across and took hold of her hand to look.

'It seems fine to me. I think you'll get away with it.'

The touch of his hand against hers made her heart start to beat with uneven heavy strokes against her chest. 'Is this charade really necessary, Luke?' she muttered as she pulled away from him.

'Maybe…maybe not. But I'm damned if I'm going to let this deal slip away just because of some quirky idea that Ron Johnson has.' Luke's eyes held with hers, a serious expression in their velvet dark depths. 'So every little helps, and this certainly can't hurt, can it?'

'That's a matter of opinion, Luke. If Ron knows you've lied to him it could hurt a great deal. And as everyone knows you are a professional bachelor, the game could be over already.'

'Well, if that's the case we'll just persuade him that I've had a change of heart.' He shrugged. 'Let's face it, it happens. Stalwart bachelors do sometimes bite the dust, fall in love and change their mind about marriage. I could have looked into your eyes and had a lightning change of character.'

'It might be more believable if you told him you'd had a brain transplant and then fallen in love,' she said derisively.

He smiled at that. 'Well, I'll grant you neither of us are the settling down type, are we? But Ron doesn't need to know that.'

She didn't answer him.

He looked at her teasingly. 'Come on, Nikki. If we do this right it'll probably swing the deal for us.'

Nikki… He had only ever called her that when they were making love. He'd whisper it in her ear… 'That was so good, Nikki…you turn me on so much…'

Just thinking about those words and the way his hands had run with silky softness over her skin made her melt inside. 'OK…OK—I said I'd do it!' She raked a hand through her hair as she tried to make the memory go away. 'But you'll have to tell the lies because I'm not going to.'

'That's OK.'

He smiled at her, that lazy lopsided smile that she knew and loved so much. She'd have done anything for him when he looked at her like that….which was really worrying.

'Thanks, Nicole,' he said softly.

'Never mind thanking me, let's just get this show on the road.'

Fifteen minutes later they were on a speedboat, skimming across the turquoise bay. The feeling was exhilarating; Nicole could taste the spray of the water on her lips and feel the warmth of the breeze against her face.

As they rounded a headland the boat slowed, and in front of them a long white beach shimmered in the evening sun. A residence stretched along its perimeter like a luxury hotel. It was ultra modern and built on two levels. It even had its own private marina at one end of the beach and an outdoor cinema with a huge screen.

'This is it—Easter Cottage. Ron's place,' Luke said as the boat drew up alongside one of the wooden jetties.

'It's the most spacious cottage I've ever seen,' Nicole said in amusement.

'Yes—if you've got to be a recluse this is the place.' Luke laughed.

As the boat docked Luke jumped off and then held out a hand to help her ashore. She would have liked to ignore the offer, but the breeze was picking up and the boat was rocking about. So, slinging the strap of her leather briefcase over her shoulder, she swallowed her pride and placed her hand in his. Unfortunately she lost her footing as she transferred her weight from the boat and ended up stumbling against him.

For a moment he held her close against him with a steadying hand, and she was achingly aware of the lean power of his body and the familiar tang of his cologne.

'Are you OK?' He bent his head and his voice sounded deep against her ear. If she moved just a fraction, her lips would be close to his.

'Yes…sorry…about that.' It took all of her self-control, but she made herself pull sharply away from him.

'Don't apologise.' He smiled at her. 'We've got an audience, so it's good to look close.'

Nicole slanted a glance past him and saw a grey-haired man of about seventy-five standing by the top of the jetty. He was smartly dressed, in a navy blue blazer and white slacks, and he was leaning on a walking stick. He waved the stick in salute as they turned to walk closer.

'Good to see you, Ron,' Luke said as he reached to shake the man's hand. 'I'd like you to meet my business associate and fiancée, Nicole Connell.'

'Delighted.' Ron smiled at her. He had very bright blue eyes that were filled with a quiet intelligence. 'You remind me of someone,' he said suddenly as his gaze moved over her face searchingly.

'Well, I know we haven't met before, Mr Johnson.' Nicole smiled at him. 'Although I do feel I know you after all the research I have put into your company.'

'Call me Ron, please,' he insisted. 'Come on up to the house. And we'll talk in comfort.'

The inside of Ron's house looked like something out of a movie set. Persian rugs covered smooth marble floors and the views out across the Caribbean from large picture windows were spectacular.

They sat in the conservatory, looking out towards the sea.

'You've got a great place here, Ron,' Luke said as he accepted a glass of iced tea from a member of staff.

'Yes, I like it. Helen and I had planned to retire here together this year but then she got ill and...it wasn't to be.'

'You must miss your wife a lot,' Nicole said with sympathy.

'Yes, it's been hard living without her.' Ron shrugged. 'But life goes on, and I have tried to keep her memory and her wishes alive—which is why I'm being very careful about whom I sell my company to.'

'You've spent a lot of time building your business up. It's understandable that you want the best deal,' Luke said with a nod.

'Not just the best deal, the *right* deal.' Ron leaned forward in his chair and looked at them earnestly. 'Which is something my lawyers don't seem to comprehend.'

'Well, the only time lawyers get emotional is when they send out their invoice,' Nicole said wryly.

Ron looked over at her and laughed. 'Exactly right, Nicole.'

'I understand your concerns, Ron,' Nicole said gently. 'In fact I think it's wonderful that you care so much about your company and feel loyalty towards your staff. Everything nowadays is so geared to profit that the important things, like loyalty and integrity, seem to have gone by the board.'

'That's right. You see, not everyone gets that.' Ron put his glass of iced tea down with a thump. 'I've been trying to get that point across to my lawyers for the past five months, but they can't seem to see it.'

Luke leaned back in his chair with a smile and watched Nicole at work. She was incredible; she practically had Ron eating out of her hand.

'Shall we go through the points that are causing you concern one by one?' Nicole started to unfasten her briefcase.

'Let's have dinner first,' Ron said. 'And you can tell me a little bit about yourselves.'

'Yes—OK.' Nicole put the briefcase down again. 'There's not much to tell, though, Ron.'

'Now, that can't be true.' Ron smiled. 'You and Luke must have lots of plans for the future.'

'Yes...lots...' Although she smiled, Luke knew Nicole well enough to know that she was rattled. She didn't want to lie to the man...she liked him.

'Where did you two meet?' Ron asked as he settled himself back in his seat.

'Well, I've worked for the Santana company for a while now. But I didn't actually meet Luke until I transferred from the London office out to Miami.'

Luke reached across and took hold of her hand. 'And what Nicole is too shy to tell you is that it was love at first sight,' he told Ron smoothly.

Nicole glanced over at him and felt her heart starting to go into overdrive. Did he have to go OTT? It was too…discomforting…

Ron nodded. 'That was how it was with Helen and I. The moment I saw her I just knew she was the one. Some things just feel right, don't you think?'

'Absolutely.' Luke's fingers stroked over Nicole's hand in a caressing and tender manner. 'I knew the moment I set eyes on Nicole that we were destined to be together. And the strange thing was that before that moment I'd been adamant that the bachelor life was for me.'

The gentle caress of his hand against hers was sending electrical darts of awareness shooting through her entire system. With difficulty she forced herself not to pull away, conscious that it might look bad, but she desperately wanted to. It was pure torture having Luke touch her, look into her eyes and say those things.

'So, have you set a date for the wedding?' Ron asked with a smile.

'Not yet,' Nicole answered firmly. 'We've got a few things to sort out first.'

'What sort of things?' Ron asked.

'Well…' Nicole shrugged; she was starting to feel out of her depth. 'This deal with you, for one. You know what it's like, Ron.' She smiled. 'We haven't got around to getting a house together yet. We've been so busy trying to put everything into order at work. There are a lot of responsibilities in running a company, as you well know.'

Ron nodded. 'Helen and I worked together, and I remember it was sometimes hard in the early days. But a word of advice, Luke. You better pin this lady down, and quickly. Nothing is more important than that!'

'You're right, Ron.' Luke squeezed Nicole's hand. 'That's exactly what I intend to do.'

CHAPTER EIGHT

'YOU were absolutely fantastic.' Luke whispered the words in her ear. His arm was around her shoulder and he squeezed her closer.

For a moment Nicole wanted to give in to the temptation and just lean against him. It was so wonderful to be close to him...and yet so painful at the same time.

They were in the boat heading back to Luke's place and the deal was signed. Nicole could hardly believe it. For five months they had been wading through red tape, and now suddenly it was over.

'I never thought he'd sign tonight!' Luke's tone was ecstatic.

'Neither did I.' She waved towards Ron, who had come down to the beach to see them off.

'You know what swung it...you telling him that we couldn't set a date for our wedding until the deal was settled! It was pure genius, Nicole. From that moment on he was putty in our hands.'

Nicole didn't reply. She was pleased the deal was signed, but as hard as she tried she couldn't summon Luke's enthusiasm. She didn't feel good about the lies they had told. She'd really liked Ron…and deep down there was a curl of guilt that wouldn't go away when she thought about how they had deceived him. Luke had played his part very well too…in fact so well that if she hadn't known better even *she* would have been convinced that he had fallen for her at first sight.

The boat pulled out across the bay and the velvet darkness of the night closed in around them. And as the lights from Easter Cottage faded Nicole forced herself to move away from Luke. Instantly she felt bereft. It would have been so easy just to stay in the circle of his arms. All evening he had been looking at her provocatively, teasing her and talking to her with velvet warmth in his voice, and it had played havoc with her emotions. All right, she knew it had been all an act for Ron's benefit…but even so she had ached inside for it to be real. And she really hated herself for that weakness.

Although it was a warm night, she shivered.

'Do you want my jacket?' Before she could refuse the offer, Luke had taken his jacket off and draped it lightly around her shoulders.

'Thanks.' She smiled at him.

'We'll open a bottle of champagne when we get back,' he said softly. 'Have a celebration.'

'Don't you feel in the slightest bit troubled about the lies we've just told?' she asked suddenly in a husky whisper.

He smiled at her. 'Nicole, all Ron was really worried about was that his precious company is in safe hands, and it is. So, no, I don't feel guilty.'

'And you will build RJ Records up, as you agreed?' she asked him sharply.

'Yes, you know my plans, Nicole.'

'I also know that in six months' time you could change your mind and tear the place apart if it suited you.'

'None of us can see into the future. But my intentions are good where that company is concerned.' Luke turned so that he could look into her eyes. It was strange, he never usually worried about what people thought of him, but he did care about Nicole's opinion. 'I may not be sentimental when it comes to business, Nicole, but I made Ron a promise and I intend to honour it.'

Nicole inclined her head. Yes, Luke *did* have integrity in business. The only intentions that were a sham were the ones he had feigned for her, she thought suddenly. And maybe that was what was really eating away at her. He had lied so convincingly about that. All that stuff about it being love at first sight, when he didn't even believe in love.

'Well, that's all right, then.' She tried to gloss over the feelings.

'Yes, it is.' He smiled at her. 'We've done it! We've pulled off the deal of the century.'

She smiled back and tried to push everything else out of her mind. He was right. The deal was done and Ron was happy. It was the culmination of months of work and it was time to celebrate.

'And you did a great job.' He leaned across and whispered against her ear, 'I couldn't have wished for a better fake fiancée.'

'Not bad for someone you were just *making do* with,' she reminded him with a raised eyebrow. And maybe she was reminding herself of that comment as well…anything to help keep her barriers up.

He smiled. 'You know I didn't mean that. You just wound me up.'

'No, *you* wound *me* up,' she said firmly.

'But we are friends again now, so it doesn't matter,' he said huskily.

She looked into his eyes.

'We are friends.' He reached out and touched the side of her face. 'Because you know that's important to me, don't you?'

The touch of his skin against hers made her tingle inside with hungry awareness.

'Yes.' She looked away from him, her heart beating uncomfortably. 'Just friends.'

To Nicole's relief they reached the shore just then, and the engine of the boat was cut. Luke stood up and took hold of her hand to help her out onto the jetty. She noticed the flash of the diamond ring on her finger as the moonlight caught it.

As she waited for him to join her on the beach she played absently with the ring, twisting it around her finger. They could never be just friends…it was an impossibility. The tug of sensuality was still there between them, twisting insidiously like a serpent ready to pounce. She reckoned he knew that as well as she did. Maybe he'd even been playing on it this evening. She had a feeling that, like a hunter, he was always ready for the kill…waiting, biding his time…

And it would be so easy to let her guard down. When he touched her she felt an ache inside that was so deep it was scary.

Flashes of lightning lit the night sky as the boat pulled out to sea again.

'There's a storm moving in,' Luke said as he turned to walk with her up the beach and into the garden.

'Yes, guess our driver today was right.' She took a deep breath of the warm night air. It was scented with jasmine. The garden looked ghostly and unreal, the crooked shadows from the moonlight distorting the bright colours, turning everything to silver and black. There was a feeling in the air of suspense…as if the flowers and the parched earth were longing for the rain. Or was that feeling of tension just inside her? she wondered as she darted a glance over at Luke and found his eyes were on her.

'Let me give you your jacket back.' She handed it over to him and watched as he slung it casually over his shoulder. Hell, but he was far, far too good-looking, she thought nervously. 'Oh, and before I forget you better have this…' She took the engagement ring off and held it out towards him.

'Give it back to me later.' He waved a hand dismissively and changed the subject. 'I still can't believe how well tonight went. Ron was completely bowled over when you came out with all those details about the company's structure, you know. You were brilliant. Just the right amount of business, teamed with just the right amount of fictional wedding day dreaminess.'

The engagement ring seemed to burn mockingly against her skin as she put it back onto her finger. 'Thanks. All part of the fake fiancée job,' she said lightly. 'You weren't so bad yourself.'

In fact, if she were being honest, Luke had been very, very impressive. He had a brain like a steel trap, she thought wryly, and yet he could be so utterly charming. Good fun as well. Over dinner they had relaxed a little, and he had told amusing anecdotes about the recording business that had really made her laugh. She had found herself just watching him, just drinking in the lean, handsome contours of his face, the dark intensity of his eyes…the sensuality of his lips…and she had wanted him so badly that she had ached.

Luke laughed. 'We are a good team, Ms Connell,' he said roguishly.

'Break open that champagne, Mr Santana,' she said, with equal flippancy.

Luke reached and took hold of her hand. 'How about we get back together again?'

The question came so quickly on the heels of their banter that it caught her by surprise.

'Luke, don't!' She pulled her hand away from his.

'Don't what?' He came to an abrupt halt beside her.

'Don't spoil a successful evening,' she said gruffly.

'I thought I was putting the perfect end to the perfect evening,' he said. 'We could have a *real* celebration, for old times' sake…'

'*Don't*, Luke.' She shook her head.

'Don't what? Don't tell you that I want you?'

Luke stared down at her. Her eyes looked almost jade-green in this light and filled with a vulnerability that seemed to kick him inside. Women never usually made him feel like this, but she brought out a strange feeling of protectiveness inside him. 'You know I'd never do anything to hurt you.' He said the words softly.

'I know.' She looked away from him. Little did he know that he *could* hurt her so…so easily…she was just too vulnerable where he was concerned.

'Hey, you know I'm not trying to get heavy here,' he said with a smile. 'We've had a real buzz out of clinching this deal, a real surge of adrenalin. And I think we should go further and really—'

'Stop it, Luke.' She cut across him fiercely. 'I want us to be businesslike and—'

'To hell with businesslike.' Luke reached for her then, and suddenly his lips were on hers. The kiss was hungry and intense and she couldn't fight it…didn't want to fight it. After an initial stunned resistance she was melting against him and kissing him back. And it was good, so good, that she felt her legs going weak beneath her, felt her whole body surging with pleasure.

'That's better!' He pulled back from her for a moment and looked down at her teasingly. 'We are so good together, Nicole…how did we drift apart this last week?'

She shook her head. 'I don't know…I just know that we shouldn't be doing this.' Her voice was a hoarse whisper in the silence of the night.

'Why?' He held her tightly. 'We are both single. We're not hurting anybody. And it feels so right when we are together, doesn't it? How can that be wrong?'

She couldn't answer that. How could she say that she loved him? He'd probably laugh. Or at the very least he would mock her.

His mouth found hers again, and softly plundered her sweetness. 'You excite me so much.'

Nicole tried very hard to pull back.

He just wants you back in his bed to satisfy his ego, she told herself fiercely. *Don't give in…don't…* But even as she was telling herself that, her body was traitorously betraying her. She was winding her arms around his neck and kissing him with a passion that was overwhelming.

For a long while they didn't talk. They were just lost in the pleasure of being back in each other's arms.

A low growl of thunder tore through the air and suddenly large raindrops started to splatter down over them. They broke apart, startled.

'Let's get out of this!' Luke took hold of her hand and they ran towards the house. But before they could get there the rain became even heavier, drenching down over them in a torrent. It was so heavy that it made Nicole gasp, and it almost obscured the house from view.

They were both out of breath and laughing as they reached the shelter of the veranda. 'Wow—look at us! We are soaked!' Nicole pushed her wet hair back from her face and glanced down at her clothes, which were sticking to her body now.

'And you still look fabulous,' he said mischievously. 'The wet T-shirt look really suits you.'

She felt a dart of embarrassment as she noticed how revealing her top was now. 'I better go and get out of these things.'

He put a hand on her arm as she made to move past him. 'I'll come and help you.'

The playful seductive tone made her pulses race in disarray. The sensible side of her was telling her that she shouldn't have kissed him, shouldn't have allowed herself to be drawn back to him. She was still leaving herself wide open to be hurt. But there was another voice inside as well, a very insistent voice that was reminding her how wonderful it was to make love with him…reminding her how much she wanted him…right now.

'Luke, nothing has changed.' She forced herself to listen to the sensible facts.

'Of course things have changed. We've got RJ; the strain of the deal has been lifted from both of us.' He reached out and touched her face. 'I know how hard you've worked on that, Nicole, and I know it's been very highly pressured.'

He was right, it *had* been high pressure, but she would rather have gone through that a million times over than go through this torment of loving him and wanting him.

'We can relax now.'

If she relaxed now she would be back to where she started…

He traced a finger softly over her trembling lips as he looked deeply into her eyes. 'I've really missed you, Nikki,' he said as he bent closer and his lips burned across her skin. 'I've missed your sensuous body…your laughter…the spark as our eyes meet across that boardroom table.'

'Luke…' Before she could form any coherent words he had covered her lips with his. His kiss was sweet, heart-rendingly tender. She had wanted him so much, for so long, and the feelings of temptation were now overwhelming…

How was it he was able to turn her on like this? She breathed deeply, trying to block out the need…but at the same time she was putting her hand in his and allowing him to lead her into the house and up the stairs to bed.

The heat of the night was intense. Nicole threw back the sheets on the bed as she listened to the storm that was raging outside. Brutal roars burst through the night air and the darkness of the room kept exploding with violent flashes of lightning.

Tomorrow they would go back to Miami and she would forget her weakness...forget that she had just spent another incredible night in Luke's arms. She squeezed her eyes tightly closed. And she *would* forget it, she told herself firmly. Because it meant nothing.

The words ran like a reassuring mantra through her mind...except that they weren't working. How could she forget something so blissfully wonderful? How could she pretend that it meant nothing when she loved him with every fibre of her soul?

Nicole turned in the bed as another flash of lightning lit the room. Luke was next to her, the sheets low on his waist. Their eyes met across the pillow and she realised he wasn't asleep either. He reached out a hand and stroked it up over her shoulder, then raked it through the thick darkness of her hair, pushing it away from her face. The touch of his hand was possessive and sexy...and it made her heart skip several beats.

'You are incredible in bed...' He smiled that half-smile that turned her on so much.

'I'm not sure what the correct response to that should be...' She smiled back at him. 'I was always told to accept a compliment gracefully, but *thank you* sounds a bit...odd, under the circumstances.'

Luke laughed a deep throaty laugh that stirred her. Then he caught hold of her hand and turned the palm upwards towards his lips to kiss it. The feeling was curiously tender.

She felt a strange reaction in the pit of her stomach, as if her heart had somersaulted down and then bounced back up.

'I don't know why we keep ending up back in bed together.' She conjured the words almost like a protective shield. 'Because it doesn't mean anything.'

He looked over at her with a teasing gleam in his eyes. 'You analyse everything too much…' He reached for her and pulled her into the warmth of his arms. 'There are times for thinking…and times when it's good just to go with the moment…give yourself up to the feeling within.' As if to prove his words, his hands moved silkily over her body.

She closed her eyes on a wave of ecstasy. He kissed her neck and then her shoulders, and a shudder of pleasure rippled through her.

A low growl of thunder tore through the air and seemed to echo the feelings of wild pleasure inside her as he rolled her over and took her one more time…

CHAPTER NINE

SOME hours later, when Luke opened his eyes, dawn had broken outside and rain was pounding heavily against the house like a continuous rolling drum.

Scenes from the night flashed through his consciousness. The way Nicole had put her hand in his and allowed him to lead her upstairs…the way they had frantically torn their wet clothes off…hardly able to wait for each other.

He had her back! An intense feeling of satisfaction raced through him—and it made him frown. His first thought should have been the satisfaction of the business deal yesterday, and yet it seemed to pale into insignificance next to the fact that he had succeeded in getting Nicole back into his arms.

Luke turned and watched her as she slept so peacefully beside him. She looked so beautiful. Her glossy dark hair had dried in curls and her skin was clear and milky-white. He noticed how long and dark her lashes were next to her skin, how the gentle curve of her sensuous mouth moved in a half-smile.

She was beautiful, and she was his again. He could relax now, get his priorities in order. He should probably make a phone call and organise the company jet to get ready to take them back to Miami. His task here was accomplished and there were a few loose ends to tie up at the office. Plus he had business to take care of at his New York office. His mind drifted ahead as he thought about what he had to do.

Nicole's eyes flickered open and connected with his. 'Hi.' She smiled sleepily.

'Hi.' He smiled back. 'How did you sleep?'

'OK…' She stretched languorously. 'How about you?'

'Best night's sleep in a week,' he said honestly.

She turned onto her side, her eyes moving over him contemplatively. 'You know, I think this is the first time we've ever woken up in the morning with each other.'

'Is it?' He looked amused, and immediately she wished she hadn't said that.

'Anyway, I suppose we should get up.'

'I suppose we should.' Luke put his hand on her arm as she made to turn away. Suddenly, despite all his earlier practical thoughts he found himself loath to let her go. 'But we do have a lot more catching up to do,' he reminded her.

'What sort of catching up had you in mind?' she asked huskily.

'Well…' He pretended to think about that for a moment, then he leaned a little closer and kissed her lips softly. 'This kind of catching up…' He breathed the words softly. The caress was gentle and sexy and infinitely pleasurable, and she found herself moving closer, winding her arms around him.

He was the one to pull back from her, and he looked deeply into her eyes for a moment. 'That was some kiss…'

'Yes.' Her heart was racing almost violently against her chest. He was right; it had been incredible—so tender and warm that it had almost seemed to sear her soul. *She loved him so much.*

'I told you the spark hadn't gone between us.' His words held an almost smug sense of satisfaction. 'What was all that nonsense about anyway?'

Alarm bells started to cut through the pleasurable mists of Nicole's thoughts. He sounded so pleased with himself…and he made it sound as if she was some kind of errant teenager he'd pulled back into line again.

'I told you what it was about,' she said numbly.

He shook his head and moved away from her. 'Well, I guess we were both under a lot of pressure with the RJ deal.' His voice was brisk. 'But things are back to how they were between us now, and that's all that matters.'

Back to how they were. Nicole could feel her body tense at those words. Obviously he assumed that because she had slept with him again that things were back on the same footing as they had been before. As far as he was concerned his ego was sated and the one that had got away was tamed.

She watched as he started to pick his clothes up from the floor, and felt a mixture of emotions. There was a part of her that wanted to say, Yes, it's great, things *are* back the way they were—because she had hated this last week without him and last night had been so wonderful. But the other part of her was angrily reminding her that things could never go back to how they were. She loved him too much for that. Even now, watching him throw his clothes on and talk in that brisk, businesslike tone, she was filled with a feeling of *déjà-vu*, and a certainty that this wasn't what she wanted. What she wanted was for him to come back into the bed and tell her he had real feelings for her… but that just wasn't going to happen.

'All in all, it's been a very successful trip.' He glanced over at her playfully, before continuing, 'I've got some loose ends to tie up in the office when we get back to Miami, and then I've got to squeeze in a trip to the New York office before the weekend. But I'll be back on Saturday. So I think our plan should be to get together on Saturday night.' He glanced over at her, and again there was that teasing, sexy expression in his dark eyes. 'For a little more catching up,' he added huskily. 'I'll book a table at Romano's—'

Hell, but he was so arrogantly self-assured. He could have at least asked if Saturday was convenient. 'Actually, Luke, I don't think that is a good idea.' She said the words quickly, before she could change her mind. She would have adored going out with him, and there was a part of her that wanted to say, Why not? Let's just leave things as they are. But she knew in her heart that she couldn't afford to allow things to drift. Nothing had changed. She would just be storing up trouble for herself if she allowed the affair to continue in the same vein, knowing how she felt.

He looked over at her. 'Well, if you don't want to go to Romano's, we could go to Luigi—'

'No, you misunderstand.' She reached for her dressing gown and got out of bed. 'I mean that things *aren't* back to how they were.'

Luke frowned.

'Last night was great…but it was a one-off.' She forced herself to sound coolly in control, but it was light years away from how she was feeling. 'We both got a bit carried away; it was a celebration after a tough deal. You said as much yourself,' she reminded him.

'Yes, I did.' Luke glared at her. He didn't need her reminding him that things were not serious! He felt as if he had just been kicked in the solar plexus, and it was not a feeling he was used to where women were concerned. 'I also made it clear that I wanted things back to how they were between us.'

'Well, it's not what I want.'

'I don't believe you,' he grated. 'Last night was more than a one-off.'

He was rewarded by a glimpse of complete vulnerability in her green-gold eyes. She wasn't as sure as she sounded.

He moved towards her. 'I realise you've been hurt in the past, Nicole, but—'

'This isn't about the past.' She cut across him forcefully. 'It's about the future.'

'So are you seeing someone else? Is that it?' Luke forced himself to ask the question, and as he did he felt an anger inside him that surprised him. If she *was* seeing some other man he wanted to physically get hold of the guy and throw him out of her life…

'No! There's no one else!' Her voice shook vehemently.

He felt a bit better at the strength of her denial. 'So are you worried the relationship might get too serious? Because I can tell you now, Nicole, that's not my style. I don't do commitment.'

Her lips twisted wryly. Did he really think he needed to point that out? She felt like saying something sarcastic, like, *You don't say?* But she controlled herself.

Instead shc forced herself to shrug and then glance at

her wristwatch. 'Actually, Luke, we really don't have time for this.'

'Oh, yes, we do.'

Deep down Luke was telling himself to just drop this now. He honestly didn't believe in analysing relationships. And if she wanted to make this just one last fling...well, he should let her. It didn't matter! Except that when he looked over at her it *did* matter...damn it!

'Look, why don't I take you out for dinner at the weekend and we can just talk...clear the air?' He sounded as if he was begging! Luke was angry with himself; he had never lowered himself to beg a woman for a date! His father had done that with his mother, when their marriage had been on the rocks, and it hadn't worked. In fact it had just made things worse.

Nicole shook her head. 'We'll never just talk...' Her voice held a slight edge. 'We'll just go to bed together and things will be the same.' And what good would talking do anyway? she thought inconsolably. One hint of the word *love* and it would all be over anyway.

Luke watched with a feeling of complete frustration as she coolly glanced at her watch. 'It's almost eight-thirty. What time do you think we should set off back to the airport?'

'For heaven's sake, Nicole...' Luke trailed off as he noticed she suddenly looked stricken. 'What's the matter?'

Nicole was looking down at her hand. There was no ring on her engagement finger! Panic zinged through her. Where on earth was Luke's ring? She didn't remember taking it off. 'Luke, I don't know how to tell you this...' She looked over at him, her eyes wide with distress.

'What?' He took a step closer.

'I think I've lost your mother's ring!'

'Oh! Is that all?' He shook his head impatiently.

'What do you mean, *Is that all*?' She stared at him. 'It was beautiful and it belonged to your mother!' Hastily she turned and started to search on the bedside table, and then along the floor by the bed. In one way, although she was horrified to have lost something that wasn't hers, it was a relief to have something else to focus on instead of the empty, aching feeling inside her.

'Nicole, you won't have lost it.' Luke's tone was nonchalant. 'You'll have taken it off and put it somewhere. We've got other things to concentrate on right now.'

She shook her head. 'I don't remember taking it off.' She raked a hand distractedly through her hair as her mind ran back over the events of the night, trying to place when she had last seen it. 'I definitely had it in the garden, because I tried to give it back to you.'

'Nicole, just forget about the ring for now.' She was really bugging him. Why wouldn't she just talk to him?

He wanted to take hold of her and force her to look at him, but before he could say or do anything further she was heading for the door.

'I'm going to go and search downstairs. It might be lying on the veranda.'

Pulling her dressing gown tightly around her, she searched the stairs on her way down, and then she looked around the hall. There was no sign of the ring.

She stepped outside onto the veranda. Despite the rain that was thundering down it was pleasantly warm. For a moment she leaned against the railing and took a deep breath of the morning air. She should never have slept with Luke last night; it had just made everything worse. She had been so weak...but she really hadn't been able to help herself.

With determination she forced herself not to dwell on emotions and just search for the ring. A black cat had taken shelter from the storm and was curled up on a cushion on one of the large wicker armchairs. She looked up curiously as Nicole searched under her chair and around the plant pots.

There was no sign of the ring.

Nicole was just debating whether to brave the rain in her dressing gown and look along the garden path when the front door opened and Luke followed her outside. He had changed and put on a pair of light blue jeans and a white T-shirt. She had never seen him dressed so casually before. The look suited him, made him look younger, and emphasised his lean hips and broad shoulders.

She tried not to be distracted by how handsome he looked. 'I'm sorry, Luke, I haven't found it.'

He took in the look of strain in her eyes. 'I told you not to worry,' he said calmly.

'Of course I'm worried!' She ran a hand abstractedly through her hair. 'I'm starting to think it might have fallen from my finger when we were running through the rain last night.'

'We'll look later.' Luke shrugged. He knew Nicole was genuinely upset about losing the ring, but he sensed there were other emotions teeming behind those beautiful eyes. 'Why don't you sit down and I'll make us some coffee?' He hesitated. Before following her downstairs he had told himself to act coolly and not pursue the issue of seeing her again. But she looked so...captivating... He felt he needed to know exactly what was going through her mind…in depth. He frowned; it wasn't like him at all! He didn't usually need to know what women were thinking. He didn't usually care to analyse emotions. But he cared about Nicole…more than he wanted to admit even to himself. He cared about what she was feeling, what she was thinking…

Before he could stop himself he was adding, 'We really need to talk.'

'Believe me, Luke, talking isn't going to help,' she grated. Then she let her breath out in a sigh. 'And, anyway, I need to find your ring.'

'The ring really isn't that important,' he muttered angrily.

Nicole had been concentrating on scanning the floor of the porch, but she looked up with a frown. 'Of course it's important. It belonged to your mother; I'm sure it's of great sentimental value apart from anything else.'

He shook his head. 'My mother took anything of any real value to her away from this house many years ago.'

The harsh sound of his words made Nicole pause. 'What do you mean?' Despite the fact that she was so anxious about the jewellery, he had her full attention now.

'I mean that my mother was a very calculating and cold woman.'

'Was she?' Nicole was totally taken aback now. 'That's not a very nice thing to say, Luke.'

He smiled at that. That was so typical of Nicole. She was so straight…so decent. 'No, but unfortunately it's the truth.' He shrugged. 'Look, if you really want to know, my parents split up when I was eleven. My father had lost all his money on a bad business deal. He nearly lost the house…nearly lost everything. And my mother…well, let's just say she liked a certain lifestyle, if you know what I mean.' His voice grated derisively. 'She walked out on the marriage. Found herself a richer guy who could keep her in the style to which she had grown accustomed.'

'And what about you?' Nicole asked quietly.

'What about me?'

'Did she take you with her?'

'Don't be silly.' Luke's mouth twisted in disdain. 'An eleven-year-old child certainly didn't fit with her new life.'

Nicole looked over at him and suddenly a lot of things fell into place. This was the reason Luke had a complete aversion towards getting tied down into a relationship, why he concentrated on business above everything else. 'I'm so sorry, Luke,' she murmured gently. 'That must have been awful for you—'

'Hey, I don't need or want your sympathy.' He cut across her quickly. 'I only told you because you're so worried about that damn ring. In all honesty my mother probably did me a huge favour when she walked away. It taught me a thing or two about relationships…and about the importance of keeping your eye firmly on business.'

'It was a hard lesson to learn at eleven.' Nicole shook her head.

'Children are resilient.' Luke shrugged. 'It was my father who really suffered. He was able to rally himself after losing his business…but I don't think he ever really got over losing his wife.'

'He never remarried?'

Luke shook his head.

'And what about your mother?'

'Oh, yes, Adrianne remarried.' Luke's lips twisted wryly. 'Three more times, to be precise. And each time to a wealthy older guy… It never ceases to amaze me how stupid men can be where a beautiful woman is concerned.'

Nicole noticed that there was no bitterness in his tone, just a mocking irony.

'So, you see, the ring is of no importance at all. It probably isn't even worth that much either—because, knowing Adrianne, she would have had it valued. Certainly all the jewellery that was in the safe went with her.'

Nicole wanted to reach out to him, put her arms around him. But she knew such a move would just make him annoyed, so she forced herself to stand where she was. 'Do you ever see her?'

'Yes, we've met a few times. It's all very civilised.' He looked as if the subject was now boring him. 'So, let's forget foolish notions about that ring…it's of no sentimental value at all, OK?'

'OK, but I'd still like to find it,' Nicole insisted.

The door opened behind him and Luke's housekeeper walked out onto the veranda. 'There is a phone call for you, Mr Santana,' she said politely. 'It's Ted Allen from your New York office.'

'Tell him I'll ring him back,' Luke grated distractedly. The last thing he wanted now was a business discussion.

'He said it was urgent,' Deloris murmured apologetically. 'Something about a crisis with a new contract?'

Luke hesitated. 'OK. Thanks, Deloris. Tell him I'll be along in a minute.'

The door swung shut as the housekeeper went to do his bidding.

'Sounds like you might have to go straight to New York.' Nicole tried to remain stoical.

'Maybe...'

'If so, I can always take a scheduled flight back to Miami and deal with the loose ends from the RJ deal.'

For a second Luke's eyes moved over her slender figure. She looked very tantalising in the white silk dressing gown, her hair flowing like liquid silk around her shoulders. She also looked fragile, like a china doll that could break very easily. Yet she was talking about business in that damn practical tone. No other woman he had ever met had given him these problems. She was an enigma, and she was driving him totally demented.

'Never mind about that...or the blasted ring,' he grated. 'Let's talk about us, shall we?'

'Us?' She looked at him through narrowed eyes.

'Yes...' For a moment he hesitated. Had that sounded a bit heavy? 'We have fun together, Nicole,' he said firmly. 'And it's not as if either of us is looking for something more...so what's the problem?'

'The problem...?' Nicole took a deep breath and her eyes moved gently over Luke's face. His expression was intensely serious. She had never seen him look like that before.

Maybe they had reached a place where only the truth would now suffice? 'All right, I suppose...if you must know...I've never really been a casual relationship type of girl...' The words just tumbled out. 'I've enjoyed what we have had,' she added huskily, 'but deep down I'm a bit old-fashioned, I guess.' She tried to make a joke, but it fell flat. Luke was now staring at her as if she were speaking with a forked tongue.

Maybe the truth hadn't been such a good idea! 'Hey, don't look so worried. I'm not saying I want to make things deep and meaningful with *you*,' she backtracked swiftly, trying to cloak her feelings and protect her pride. 'I know *you* are not into commitment. What we had was just a fling. I know that. But I need to move on now.'

When Luke still didn't say anything, she continued swiftly, 'So, you see, talking isn't going to help.'

'I see.' Now Luke looked totally disconcerted. 'I didn't spot that coming.'

'Neither did I, to be honest.' Nicole forced herself to sound casual. 'Anyway…' she said crisply. 'You go and take your phone call. And I'll go and pack my bags.'

Somehow she managed to smile, and with her head high she moved past him and back into the house.

Her heart was racing against her chest. She felt sick. She shouldn't have said all that!

But after he had told her about his mother, somehow she just hadn't been able to lie to him any more in that flippant tone. She had thought it was better to be honest.

Big mistake! As soon as she had seen the perplexed look on his face she had known she had stepped on a landmine! At least she had thought on her feet and he didn't know she had fallen in love with him. That would have been too embarrassing. She needed to leave herself with some dignity.

Nicole sat down on the edge of the bed. Suddenly she was feeling very ill. What was causing that? she wondered. Emotional upset? She couldn't still be suffering from food poisoning…could she?

She sat for a few moments longer, but instead of feeling

better she started to feel worse. The queasy feeling intensifying, she dashed for the sanctuary of her *en-suite* bathroom.

Half an hour later, as she lay weakly on the bed, she found Luke's ring lying under the sheet. It must have fallen off when they were making love. She turned it in her hand, watching how it sparkled in the morning light. At least she now knew why Luke was so determined to avoid any lasting intimacy.

Not that it changed anything, she thought sadly. With determination she got up. There was no point lying here trying to question things. She should shower and change and pack her bag.

A little while later Nicole went back downstairs. She had dressed in a pale blue summer dress and her hair and make-up were perfect. She was determined that there would be no chink in her armour when she faced Luke.

He was making another phone call; she could hear his crisp, businesslike tones drifting down the hallway from the study.

'Would you like some breakfast, Ms Connell?' Deloris appeared from the kitchen.

The mere thought of eating made Nicole's stomach turn in disapproval. 'No, thanks, Deloris, I'll just have a glass of water.'

Luke looked up as she appeared in the doorway. 'I've decided that Ted Allen is totally useless when it comes to anything urgent!' he grated as he put the phone down. 'You were spot on. I *am* going to have to get to New York straight away!'

She smiled. 'You just like to be in control,' she observed softly.

For a moment Luke leaned back in his chair. She was right. In fact she knew him very well…maybe better than any woman before. The knowledge added to what she had said earlier and intensified the feeling of disquiet inside him. Nicole wasn't the sort of woman you just had a fling with. *Why hadn't he seen that before?* He frowned. Maybe he *had* seen it, and he had just ignored it because it was too disconcerting. He didn't want a serious relationship… the very words were an anathema to him.

'Yes, you're right; I *do* like to be in control. And I can't trust Ted Allen to sort this out on his own.' He forced himself to concentrate on the business in hand. 'The fact is that I'll probably be stuck out there for a week at this rate.'

'That's no problem. As I said, I'll deal with the remainder of the paperwork for RJ.'

She was fabulous, Luke thought as his eyes drifted over her. So cool and poised and yet inside so decent and— He switched his thoughts off abruptly and stood up. 'I've managed to get you on the next available flight to Miami. It leaves at midday.'

'That's good. Will your driver be able to take me to the airport, or shall I get a taxi?' she asked briskly.

'My driver will take you.' Luke sat down on the edge of the desk and looked over at her. 'About what you were saying earlier…' he began cautiously.

'Listen, Luke, we don't need to go through that again.' She intersected him hurriedly. She really didn't want to talk about anything personal now. She was holding herself together on the slimmest of control lines as it was. 'As you said yesterday, we're friends and good work colleagues.'

Luke frowned. 'Yes…yes, we are,' he agreed in a firm

tone. 'And when I get back to Miami maybe we can still have dinner?' He folded his arms.

She shook her head and swallowed. 'Not a good idea, Luke.'

The silence between them seemed loaded with some kind of emotion that twisted inside Nicole, inflicting even more pain.

'Your taxi is here, Mr Santana.' Deloris appeared in the doorway.

'OK—thanks, Deloris.' Luke glanced at his watch. 'I've got the company jet waiting, so I'd better go, Nicole.'

She forced herself to smile brightly at him. 'Yes—you have a good flight.'

As Luke stood up and walked over towards her she could feel herself tremble inside.

'You take care of yourself.' He touched her face lightly, and for a moment looked into her eyes. Then he was gone.

CHAPTER TEN

NICOLE returned from Barbados and threw herself into her work. On her first day back a bouquet of flowers arrived for her. It was hand-tied and magnificent.

'Gosh, they are really beautiful,' Molly said as she handed them across to her.

'Yes...' Nicole's heart thundered hopefully as she buried her face for a moment in the sweet peppery scent. Maybe Luke had gone to New York and had a rethink... Maybe he missed her... Cutting her thoughts abruptly, she opened the accompanying card.

Thanks for everything. Luke.

She stared at the card in utter disappointment. But in reality it had been absurd to expect anything else.

'Got an admirer?' Molly asked inquisitively.

'No, they're just from Luke, thanking me for my work on the RJ takeover.' She handed them back to her secretary. 'You deal with them, will you?'

'Yes, of course. How lovely of him!'

'Yes...lovely.'

After that she tried very hard not to think about Luke at all.

A week went by, and apart from one phone call from him to check on the loose ends from the RJ deal there was no further contact. According to the gossip around the office he seemed firmly ensconced in the New York office and might be there for some time.

Probably just as well, she told herself firmly as she remembered their stiltedly polite telephone conversation. If speaking to him were difficult, then seeing him would be even worse. Yet, no matter how many times she told herself that, she still missed him.

In spite of the fact that she no longer had to worry about the RJ deal, things were pretty hectic in the office. Nicole had a lot of work to do on new contracts, and her days seemed to be getting longer and longer. So she supposed it wasn't strange that she should feel tired, but what was strange was the fact that she was still suffering from nausea.

She had been so sick this morning that she had hardly been able to drag herself into work. And by mid-morning she felt so bad that she had to phone the doctor for an appointment.

'Will you cancel my appointments from three-thirty onwards tomorrow?' she asked her secretary as she brought some mail in for her. 'I've got a doctor's appointment and I'm not sure how long I'll be.'

'OK.' Molly glanced over at her with sympathy. 'You do look very pale.'

'I feel a bit better at the moment, actually.' Nicole went through her correspondence with a brisk efficiency. 'But this seems to be the pattern. I think I'm feeling better and then, whoosh, it's back again the next day.'

'My sister is like that at the moment. But then she's pregnant.' Molly laughed. 'It's not morning sickness, is it?'

'I think that's one thing I can definitely rule out,' Nicole said firmly. 'Did you manage to get Bob Tate on the phone, by the way?' she asked as Molly headed back to her own office.

'Yes, he said it was all in hand. And the recording studio is booked for the day.'

'Great.'

'Oh, and by the way,' Molly added casually, 'Luke is back from New York. I've just seen him in the corridor.'

Nicole tried not to react to this piece of information, but it rippled through her in shock waves. Luke was back! Just knowing that he was in the building filled her with a sense of excitement...and a sense of sadness as well. He'd obviously walked right past her office and hadn't even come in to say hello. But then why should he? She had made it clear that she wasn't going to sleep with him again, and he'd probably moved on. All that talk about being friends was rubbish.

With determination she continued with her work. But it was difficult to concentrate now. She longed to see him...

Although she had tried not to think about him since returning home, in reality he had filled her mind. She remembered the look in his eyes when he'd told her about his parents splitting up. She imagined him as a vulnerable eleven-year-old in that house in Barbados, abandoned by his mother, imagined his loneliness and his feeling of helplessness as he watched his father fall apart.

No wonder he was so focused on business and so flippant with women. Nicole felt for him. She really did. But the worst thing she could do was to feel sorry for him. Luke didn't want her sympathy, and she had to remember that.

Even so, she itched to pick up the phone now and make up some excuse to speak to him. She clenched her hands and forced herself not to do any such thing! If their last telephone conversation were anything to go by it would only be a stilted and wooden exchange anyway.

By five o'clock she couldn't stand it any longer and packed up her papers. 'I'm going to finish this paperwork at home, Molly.' She put her head around her secretary's door.

'Not feeling well?' Molly asked with concern.

'No, not really.' It was as good an excuse as any, Nicole thought as she headed down towards the lifts. In fact she felt all right. At least she didn't want to throw up—and for the first time in ages she felt hungry.

As there was nothing in her apartment to eat, she stopped off at the local store and as usual hurriedly shoved a few things in a basket. As she stood by the till, waiting to be served, she glanced down at her purchases and was struck by how strange they were. She never usually ate chocolate ice cream, or pistachio nuts or olives…

Heck, if she ate the combination that was in that basket, she would *deserve* to be sick tomorrow!

It's not morning sickness, is it? Molly's teasing words flashed through her mind.

Now she came to think about it, her period *was* late. *But she couldn't be pregnant.* It wasn't possible. And anyway, she and Luke had always made love responsibly.

It was her turn to be served and she moved to put her

basket on the counter. *Except there was that one time a while ago, when they'd had an accident.*

The memory zinged into her mind and she felt herself freeze. *No, she couldn't be…* But even so she heard herself saying to the assistant, 'I've forgotten something. Could you put my basket to one side, please? I'll be back in a minute.'

'Sure.' The basket was removed, and Nicole found herself walking down the aisles towards the pharmacy.

She stood for a while in front of the pregnancy testing kits. There had been a time in her life when she had bought those regularly. And the results had always been negative. She couldn't look at them on the shelf now without remembering her many disappointments. What were the chances of her being pregnant after one accident when she had spent so long trying for a baby with her husband?

It would probably be a waste of time even trying a test. But even so… Just to eliminate the possibility from her mind she reached and took one of the boxes off the shelf.

When Nicole got back to her apartment she made herself something to eat and then finished off the paperwork from that afternoon. But even as she was ploughing through her work she was conscious of that test kit, waiting for her in the bathroom cabinet.

By nine o' clock she couldn't put it off any longer…

'Yes, I can confirm that your test was correct. You are pregnant, Nicole. Probably about six weeks, I would say.'

The doctor's words thundered through Nicole's mind as she left his surgery and got into a cab. But she still could hardly believe it.

Last night when she had done the test and it had been positive, she had convinced herself that the result was a mistake.

All that time of trying, longing to be pregnant…and suddenly it had just happened, when she least expected it. She had said that to the doctor and he had just smiled and shrugged. 'Sometimes that is the way it happens.'

Nicole stared sightlessly out at the Miami streets, at the bright sunshine reflecting on the glass windows of the Art Deco buildings.

She was still in a state of shock.

'You might have been very tense and stressed when you were trying for a baby before,' the doctor had said nonchalantly. 'And this time you were relaxed. That can make a difference.'

She had certainly felt relaxed around Luke. The chemistry between them had been much more powerful than it had ever been with Patrick. In fact if she were really honest she had never felt the same depth of emotion for Patrick as she had for Luke. Yes, she had loved him…but it had been a different kind of love. She had found herself trying to please Patrick, and had felt that she'd never really succeeded because he had always made it clear that it was her fault they had no family.

They had got to the point where nothing she had done was right. She remembered she had suggested they adopt and he had been furious. The idea had been completely abhorrent to him. She realised now that their relationship had been hollow…Patrick had only truly loved himself.

Luke, on the other hand, had been a wonderfully considerate lover. He had also been responsible enough to mention the morning after pill when that condom had broken, she reminded herself fiercely.

'Don't worry about it,' she had murmured as she watched him getting dressed to leave. 'I'll deal with it.'

The words echoed in her mind now. *She really had meant to deal with it.* But that day had been doubly hectic. There had been numerous meetings, there'd been people bombarding her from all sides with e-mails and questions, and by the time she'd got to the end of that day she had felt as if her head was exploding. The morning after pill had been the last thing on her mind. And if she were honest she hadn't really worried about it at all. She hadn't felt she needed to take that pill because the fact was that she had been married to Patrick for five years and for eighteen months of that time they had been desperately trying for a baby…with no success.

But now here she was…pregnant. It was like a miracle.

Butterflies of excitement stirred inside her. She knew that she was on her own and this wasn't an ideal situation. Luke didn't want any kind of commitment, and a child was the biggest commitment of all! But she had longed for a baby for so long that she couldn't help but feel thrilled.

Her baby would not have a father, but she had enough love inside her to make up for that. She knew she would cope…knew she would make a good mum.

But what should she say to Luke? The question caused the butterflies to flutter a little more fiercely inside. He would be furious!

Maybe the best thing to do would be to hand in her notice and go back home to England without telling him about the baby. She had a friend in London who had started her own business, and she had talked in the past about offering Nicole a job. Plus, she would have her parents around for support. They would be over the moon to be grandparents.

All things considered, going home was probably the most sensible thing. If she left the company Luke wouldn't need to know that he was a dad. She would just never see him again.

The thought caused regret to ricochet inside her. But she quickly buried it.

Leaving without telling him she was pregnant was the best thing all round. He'd only be furious when she told him how much she wanted the baby. It could turn into a very unpleasant situation, with him blaming her for not taking the morning after pill. There was no point in even having that conversation. She didn't need Luke anyway. She was an independent modern woman and she would manage perfectly on her own. This was *her* baby.

The taxi pulled up outside her office block and Nicole got out. As she walked inside and got into the lift she was still planning her future. Back in London she could find a lovely downstairs apartment… That would be easier with a pram…

'Ah, there you are, Nicole.' Molly's friendly tones cut into her daydreams.

Nicole took a hasty step back and looked in through the open door of her secretary's office. To her surprise, her eyes met directly with Luke's. The connection caused a jolt of electricity to sizzle through her.

He was perched on the edge of Molly's desk, and it looked as if they'd been having a relaxed conversation. 'Hello, Nicole,' he said quietly.

'Hi.' She tried very hard to gather her scattered wits. 'I didn't expect to see you.'

'I got back from New York yesterday.'

She nodded. 'Good trip, I hope?'

'Yes, it was fine.'

There was silence for a moment and as she looked at him Nicole could feel the ache of missing him like a tangible force.

'Anyway, Luke, I've got rather a lot to do, so I'd better get on…' She was suddenly desperate to get away.

'Actually, I wanted a word with you.' Luke stood up. 'We'll talk in your office.'

'Oh…OK.' She shrugged. Even though she sounded casual her heart was turning over. Being around him was so hard…especially now, with her secret burning inside her. 'I think I've got ten minutes…haven't I, Molly?' She glanced pointedly over at her secretary.

Molly looked at her blankly. There were no appointments in the book because Nicole had asked her to cancel everything for the rest of the afternoon. So really she could spend whatever time she wished with Luke.

'My next appointment is due in about ten minutes, isn't it?' Nicole prompted her sharply.

'Oh…yes!' Molly finally took the hint and nodded.

'I thought so,' Nicole continued briskly. 'Come through, Luke.'

She led the way into her office and then, closing the door behind them, made her way round to sit behind the safety of her desk.

In contrast to how *she* was feeling, she noticed how relaxed Luke was as he sat opposite. He was wearing a dark suit and a pale blue shirt that was open at the neck, and he looked impossibly handsome. Just looking at him made her heart race a little faster, made her remember what it was like to lie in his arms and be held close.

'Before I forget, Aaron Williams has had some trouble with one of the contracts I need to deal with...' Nicole flicked through some paperwork sitting next to her and tried to focus on business. 'Yes, here we are...it's for the new group we want—'

'I'll go up and talk to Aaron about it later.' Luke cut across her. He leaned back in his chair and fixed her with that steady look that she found so unnerving. 'Molly tells me you've just had some time off to go to the doctor,' he said suddenly. 'I'm sorry to hear that you've been ill.'

'Oh, that! It was nothing.' Nicole waved a hand airily and hoped her voice was steady. 'I feel much better now.' She imagined that she could feel Luke's dark gaze burning into her, and that he knew the truth... Which of course he couldn't possibly... But even so she could feel her temperature rising.

Didn't he deserve to know the truth? a little voice suddenly asked inside her. Did she really have the right to keep the fact that he was going to be a dad from him?

Hastily she cut those thoughts dead. *He wouldn't want to know...*

'Well, I'm glad to hear it.' Luke smiled. 'But if you need some time off work, that's not a problem,' he added.

'Luke, I'm fine.' Was it her imagination, or were his eyes moving almost searchingly over her features? Hastily she changed the subject. 'So...was there something *about business* that you wanted to talk about?' She forced a bright and efficient tone into her voice and glanced at her watch.

When she glanced back at him, she could see a glint of impatience in his dark eyes.

'Listen, Nicole, you can drop the pretence,' he grated suddenly.

'What pretence?' She felt the colour drain from her face.

'I know the truth.'

The blunt words made Nicole's heart stop beating for an instant. She stared at him in horror. How could he know? She'd only just found out herself! 'What are you talking about, Luke?' Her voice came out in a croak.

'I'm talking about the fact that you have no appointment. I've just looked in your diary, for heaven's sake!'

'Oh!' She felt her breath come out in a rush, felt almost weak with relief. 'Well, I *am* busy, Luke. I've just taken a few hours off, and the work doesn't go away.'

'Yes…whatever.' Luke cut across her, his voice harsh. 'Look, I've got a few details to discuss with you. But as you are so obviously overstretched we'll discuss them later.'

'Yes, if it's not important business, then that would be better.' Nicole grabbed the opportunity.

'Fine, I'll ring you later.' His eyes seemed to cut into hers.

Nicole nodded. Then watched as he turned and walked out of the room. He closed the door with a firm thud behind him.

Nicole bit down on her lip. This situation wasn't good. And the longer she left it the worse it was going to get, she told herself sensibly. The only thing she could do was to give in her resignation. And she would have to do it straight away.

With determination she turned towards her computer, opened a new blank document and started to type. She would get Molly to bring it upstairs just at the close of day.

CHAPTER ELEVEN

It was six-thirty and Luke was still sitting at his desk. He was furious with himself. Nicole was starting to become an obsession, he told himself angrily.

All the time he had been in New York he hadn't been able to get her out of his head. All week he had thought about her…her beautiful body…her soft skin…her eyes…her smile… And every woman he looked at he'd compared with her and found them lacking. When he had phoned her to talk about the remaining aspects of the RJ deal it had been pure torture, because he'd had to force himself not to let the conversation veer towards anything too personal.

It had been the same yesterday. As soon as he had got back into the office he had gone down to her floor to see her. And then he'd stopped himself. Because he didn't have any business to discuss with her. Anything he said to her would have been of a personal nature. And that wasn't right. Nicole was off limits, he'd told himself. She was in the past.

She wanted to move on to something more serious and he just wasn't cut out for that kind of a relationship. He was the carefree bachelor type, for heaven's sake. He liked to enjoy himself!

Trouble was, he wasn't really enjoying himself. In desperation he'd gone out on a date last night, to try and clear Nicole out of his mind. But the strategy hadn't worked. He hadn't been able to find any enthusiasm for the woman… and yet she had been gorgeous and entertaining and more than willing to go to bed with him. So why had he turned her down? Why had he gone back to his flat early, alone and morose?

So today, unable to bear it, he had breezed down to Nicole's office. All right, he didn't want a serious relationship—but that was OK, wasn't it? Because she had made it clear she didn't want one with *him*…just with someone else. So why couldn't they just continue to see each other until the time when she *did* find someone else?

It seemed a simple enough option…and they *had* agreed that they were going to be friends…

Except, once again, Nicole was treating him with cool disdain.

And she'd looked so pale. Maybe he should have insisted that she took a few days off. She had been working very hard.

Now he was worrying about her! The woman was driving him crazy. How on earth was he going to get her out of his system?

There was a tap at his door and Sandy, his PA, came in. 'I'm going to get off now, Luke,' she said with a smile.

'Yes, of course. Sorry, Sandy, I didn't realise you were still here.'

'That's OK; I was doing a bit of catching up. Oh, and Nicole's secretary brought these up a while ago.'

She put two letters down onto his desk.

'Thanks, Sandy.' Luke picked them up and opened

them. The first was a memo on the details of the troublesome contract that Nicole had mentioned to him earlier. His eyes flicked over it with little interest.

The second was Nicole's letter of resignation. Luke stared down at it in complete and utter shock!

Nicole had luxuriated in a long, relaxing bath, and now she was curled up on the sofa in her dressing gown, listening to some music. She'd lit some candles along the mantelpiece and she was enjoying some ice cream. All things considered, she felt quite good.

True, she had just given up her dream job. But she was pregnant…and that was the one thing in life that she had always wanted. So she had no real regrets.

She'd had no choice anyway. She couldn't stay here and work for Luke whilst having his child…it would be too awkward a situation. And if she had asked to be transferred to the London office that wouldn't have worked either, because Luke would have found out about the baby through the grapevine. And, all right, he couldn't force her to have an abortion…but he could make life very difficult. Plus there would be the torture of seeing him…watching as he got on with his life and dated other women. She didn't think she could bear it. Today when she had seen him in the office she had just ached for him…

Swiftly she turned her mind away from that and tried to think positively. You couldn't have everything in this life, and being back in London would have its compensations. Her parents would be nearby, and there was the opportunity of another job…it would be fine.

She didn't need Luke.

She stretched and turned on one of the lamps next to her, and then picked up a magazine on pregnancy that she had bought on her way home from work.

The shrill ring of the front doorbell shattered the silence.

Nicole looked up with a frown. Who could that be? she wondered. As she was in her dressing gown, and not expecting anyone, she decided not to answer it. She continued to read.

The bell rang again, and then a few seconds later someone rapped loudly on the door. Maybe it was one of her neighbours, Nicole thought suddenly. Maybe there was something wrong…it sounded quite urgent. Putting her magazine down, Nicole tightened the belt of her dressing gown and went to investigate.

She opened the door a couple of inches and peered out.

Her eyes widened in surprise when she saw Luke standing on her doorstep. 'What on earth are *you* doing here?'

'I think you know!' He put one hand against the door and opened it wider, then strode past her into the lounge without even waiting to be asked. 'We need to have words.'

'This really isn't a good time.' She ran after him in consternation.

'No?' His eyes flicked around the room, taking in the low lighting and the candles, and then lingering on her. She looked fabulous in that black silk robe; it dipped at her neckline, giving just a hint of the firm curve of her breast. Her hair was tousled and sexy, her skin held a flare of heat over her high cheekbones, and her eyes sparked with green fire. 'Are you expecting someone?'

'No! I'm having a relaxing evening.' She glared at him angrily. 'Not that it's any of your business!'

She was right—it wasn't any of his business. Luke tried to calm down, but he was filled with anger. He watched as she moved towards the sofa and straightened the cushions. It looked as if she was hiding something behind one of them.

'Look, I realised this isn't a good time—but there never seems to be a good time, does there? I tried to talk to you this afternoon, but you were too busy.'

Nicole crossed the room and turned the music off. 'What is this about, Luke?'

Her calmness really infuriated him. 'Why the hell didn't you tell me that you wanted to quit your job when we spoke earlier?'

'Oh! You've received my resignation, then?' She ran her hand down over the silk of her robe.

'Yes, of course I've received it!' He glared at her. 'Why didn't you tell me to my face this afternoon that you wanted to leave?'

'I thought it was more professional to put it in writing.' She moistened her lips nervously. 'And, as you have just pointed out, I was very busy this afternoon. It wasn't a good time.'

He looked at her through narrowed eyes. 'So why do you want to leave?'

'Luke, I don't really want to discuss this right now.'

'Well, I do.' He took a step nearer.

She sat down on the sofa. 'I want to go back to London.'

'Have you been offered another job?' Luke moved and stood in front of the fireplace, glowering at her.

She felt as if she was being interrogated, and she didn't like it. 'You know what, Luke? That really isn't any of your business.' She said the words quietly. 'I've behaved in a businesslike way, I've given you the required amount of notice, and that's all that should matter.'

'Well, I think I deserve more!'

'Why?'

The calm question threw him. 'Well, because we had more than a businesslike relationship, for one thing...and for another I thought we were friends.'

'It's nothing personal.' Nicole had to look away from him now, because her cool composure was cracking a little. Who was she kidding? *Nothing personal?* This was as personal as it could get. 'I just think it's time I went home.'

The silence in the room suddenly seemed so heavy that she could hear the clock ticking on the mantelpiece as if it had been magnified a hundred times.

'And you couldn't tell me to my face?'

Why did he keep harping on about that? Nicole raked a hand impatiently through her hair. 'I told you...I thought it was best to keep things on a businesslike footing.'

'OK.' Luke leaned one hand against the fireplace. 'So let's cut to the chase, shall we? How can I persuade you to stay?' he asked briskly. 'How about a pay rise? And I'll throw in some shares...'

He sounded so calm and confident. Luke always got what he wanted, she thought as she looked at him, but not this time. She shook her head. 'This isn't about money, Luke. This is about what is best for me in the long term.'

'Is this because you haven't been feeling well?' he asked suddenly. 'Are you all right?'

The sudden deep concern in his tone was nearly her undoing.

'I told you, I'm fine.'

'But you haven't been feeling well, have you?' His voice held a sudden note of insight. 'Maybe what you need is a break.' He stepped away from the fireplace and came to sit next to her on the sofa. 'I've got a house down in Key West. It's really beautiful down there. Why don't you take a trip, have a week off, laze by the pool in the sun and just think about things?'

'Thanks, Luke.' She shook her head. 'But that's not going to help.'

'It might do you good.' He smiled at her. 'And at the end of the week I could jump on the company jet and come down and see you. We could just chill out together and talk.'

His gentle velvety tone was infinitely sexy, and as she looked into the darkness of his eyes she was almost tempted to say yes. But what would it solve? She would just be prolonging things. And when she went back to work nothing would have changed except for the fact that her pregnancy would be further advanced.

There was no time to put things off, she told herself. She shook her head. 'Thanks for the offer, Luke, but I've made my mind up.'

'And there's nothing I can say to make you change it?'

She shook her head.

'I see.' Luke's glance moved from her towards the coffee table. He noted the tub of ice cream, and there was a china dish of pistachio nuts, some black olives and a bowl of cherries. 'That's a strange combination.'

'What?' Nicole felt herself stiffen.

'The food.'

'I'm just unwinding, Luke.' She shrugged. 'I think you should go now.'

He transferred his attention back to her face. But he made no attempt to move. He was only inches away from her, and she could see the flecks of gold in the darkness of his eyes.

'I don't want you to go back to London, Nicole.' He said the words quietly, and there was a deep sincerity in them that melted her heart. She didn't want to go either. She would have given anything to just lean a little closer and go into his arms. To give up all pretence of being strong and in control…

This was the father of her child. The words echoed inside her. Maybe if she told him the truth…

'Apart from anything else, you are invaluable to the company here.'

His words were like a cold splash of water. Luke's main concern was always business. Nothing would ever change that. 'Well, you know what they say, Luke. No one is irreplaceable.' She moved further away from him.

'So they say.' His eyes raked over her face. 'Are you leaving because of our relationship?'

The softly asked question ricocheted through her. 'What relationship would that be?' she muttered flippantly.

'You know what I mean.'

She shook her head. 'You think everything revolves around you, don't you, Luke? Honestly, sometimes you can be insufferably arrogant.'

He smiled at that. 'Just checking.'

Fleetingly she was lost in that smile. Sometimes when he looked at her in a certain way…like now, for instance…

she felt a sudden flare of longing that overwhelmed everything else.

'Well, now you've checked I think you should go.' She forced herself to say the words.

Instead of moving, he leaned back against the cushions of the sofa. 'Aren't you going to offer me a drink before I go? That's not very hospitable of you, Nicole.'

'Yes, well, I'm not feeling particularly hospitable.'

'I'll just have a coffee, and then I'll get out of your way.' He didn't budge.

She stared at him. Heavens, but the man was infuriating.

He raised an eyebrow and gave her that mocking smile she knew so well.

Obviously he didn't care that she didn't want him here. She shook her head. 'One coffee and then I want you to go,' she warned him shakily.

'Thanks. Black, no sugar…in case you've forgotten.'

'I hadn't forgotten.' She turned and went into the kitchen.

It was damn ironic that when she had wanted him to hang around here he wouldn't, and now that she wanted him to go he was making himself comfortable on the sofa! Nicole wished she'd thought to hide that pregnancy magazine before she opened the front door. She'd managed to shove it behind one of the cushions, but it was hardly the safest of places.

Nicole switched on the kettle and got some cups out of the cupboard. Then she stood and tried to compose herself. She would chat politely with him and then show him the door…no distractions…that was final. And she was doing the right thing not telling him about the baby.

As soon as Nicole disappeared into the kitchen Luke

searched behind the cushions to find what she had hidden. He really didn't know what he had expected to find, but it certainly wasn't a magazine about pregnancy! He stared at it, completely dumbfounded. Then his gaze moved towards the table and the strange combination of food. He felt a rising sense of what could only be described as panic. It was the same sensation he had felt when he had read Nicole's resignation, and it was a whole new experience for him.

Was *this* why Nicole was leaving? His mind flicked back to what Molly had told him today about Nicole being ill...then there was her trip to the doctor.

Had she lied to him when she had told him there was nothing wrong? With a feeling of grim determination he stood up and went through to the *en suite* bathroom off her bedroom. His eyes raked along the shelves; there was nothing there apart from the normal beauty products and bath foams. He didn't really know what he was looking for, just some other conclusive proof, and as he glanced at the open bathroom cabinet there it was. An empty box for a pregnancy testing kit.

Nicole was pouring Luke's coffee when he appeared behind her in the kitchen doorway.

'So...interesting choice of reading material.'

His dry tone made her swivel around.

He was leaning against the doorframe, watching her through narrowed eyes. 'Care to explain?' Although his voice was light, one look at his face made her stomach start to knot with dread.

'Sorry?' Instinct told her to play this very carefully. Best to pretend she didn't know what he was talking about. 'Explain what?'

Luke took a step further into the room and to her consternation tossed the magazine down on the kitchen table with a less than good-humoured thud.

'Oh, that!' Nicole glanced down at the glossy page, with its picture of a pregnant mother, and cringed. What on earth had possessed her to buy that? 'It's not mine. A friend left it behind last week.'

She could see anger in the darkness of his eyes now. And as he stepped further into the room Nicole took an instinctive step back.

'I suppose this isn't yours either?' The box from her pregnancy testing kit followed the magazine down onto the table.

'Where the hell did you get that?' To her dismay her voice wasn't at all steady now.

'It was sitting in your bathroom cabinet.'

'How dare you go through my things?'

He just looked at her with dark, disdainful eyes. 'You've lied to me!' He came closer.

'Luke, you are scaring me!' Without realising it she had backed into the countertop behind her and couldn't get any further away from him.

'Only for the fact that you are *pregnant*… I'd say good.'

For a fleeting second she wondered if she could still lie her way out of this, tell him the box wasn't hers either. But, judging by the harsh expression on Luke's face, she would probably just make things worse. He wasn't going to be receptive to any more lies.

Luke watched the shadows flicking through her green eyes. 'Haven't you got anything to say?'

She raised her chin a little higher. 'You've no right to come round here, prying into my life!'

'Well, it's a damn good job I did!' he growled. 'Because you *had* no right to keep this from me. I presume it's my baby?'

'Of course it's your baby!' Nicole swallowed hard on a knot of anger and tried to keep her nerve.

'So how many weeks pregnant are you?' Luke demanded.

When she didn't answer him immediately he put one hand on the counter behind her, effectively trapping her.

'Six weeks!' she answered hurriedly.

He pulled back and looked furious. 'Six weeks and you didn't mention anything!'

She raked an unsteady hand through her hair. 'I've only just found out. I had it confirmed by the doctor today. I didn't tell you because it wouldn't have served any purpose.'

'Oh, really? And you decided this all by yourself?'

Nicole tried to ignore the cutting sarcasm in his tone. 'Yes.' She angled her chin up firmly. 'I don't want you to concern yourself with this, Luke. It's my business and I'll take care of it.'

'Take care of it?' His eyes narrowed on her face. 'Are you thinking—?'

'No, I am not!' She cut across him, her eyes wide with horror as she realised he was about to mention termination. 'I want this baby with all my heart.' Her voice trembled slightly.

'I see.' He seemed to relax for a moment, and then he started to pace up and down beside her.

'What I'm saying is that it's *my* responsibility,' she added tersely.

'So what are you telling me? That you made medical history and conceived all by yourself? You better think again about that.' Luke swung around to face her again and his voice was very cold now. 'Because, if my memory serves me correctly, six weeks would just fit in with the night when a wild episode in your bed led to my suggesting the morning after pill.' He noticed how the pallor of her skin suddenly flared with incriminating colour. 'I take it you didn't follow my advice?'

A long silence stretched between them. She could feel Luke's eyes boring into her with deep intensity.

'Nicole, I asked you a question.' He took a step closer, and now he was so near that he was within a whisper of her. She could feel the heat from his body, smell the scent of his cologne. It brought back memories of their last night together… She remembered how he had made her feel…how he had caressed her, held her, stroked her.

'Nicole?' The coldness of his tone was a million miles away from the passion of that night.

'No.' Nicole made the admission huskily. 'No I didn't take your advice.'

'So you deliberately went against my wishes,' he said calmly.

She didn't answer him…couldn't answer him.

'Have you just used me as a sperm bank?'

The angry question shocked her. 'No! No, Luke—of course not!'

He coldly watched the play of emotions in her eyes. 'Well, from where I'm standing that is what it looks like. And I am not happy about it, Nicole.'

She looked horrified. 'Luke, really! No matter what else you might think, I didn't plan for this to happen!'

'So, as a matter of interest, why didn't you take that pill?'

The calm question made her temper flare. 'Because I didn't think I could get pregnant. So I didn't worry about it.' She glared at him, her eyes over-bright with emotion. 'My ex-husband and I tried for a long time to have a baby. It's what eventually broke us apart…' Her voice wobbled precariously. 'He now has a two-and-a-half-year-old little girl. So I never thought in a million years that when we had one little accident I would get pregnant. How could I, after all that time of trying…of hoping? So how dare you talk to me like this? How dare you accuse me of something so…so…?'

He reached out a hand and touched her arm, but she shrugged him away. 'I have every right to be angry, Nicole.' Although he said the words firmly, his tone was softer now. 'You should have told me!'

'Told you what? That I thought I couldn't get pregnant?' Her voice trembled. 'That was really none of your business. We were having sex, Luke, not a relationship.'

'Don't be sarcastic, Nicole.'

As she looked up she could see a pulse ticking in the side of his jaw, and his eyes were dark with fury.

'I meant you should have told me that you were pregnant.'

'There was no point.' She held his gaze firmly.

'No point?' He looked as if he was having difficulty reining back his temper again. 'I'm the baby's father. Of course there was a point! We need to discuss this.'

'There is nothing to discuss. I'm not going to have an abortion, Luke, and that's final.' Her heart was thundering against her chest so hard it was making her feel ill. 'I told you. I want this baby.'

He stared at her for a moment. 'It sounds like you've got everything all worked out.'

'Yes, I have.' She held his dark gaze steadily. 'I didn't plan it...but I've had time to think about it and work out what I'm going to do. All I'm saying is that *you* don't need to worry. I don't want anything from you...either emotionally or financially. I'll be absolutely fine. That's why I didn't tell you.'

'And I take it this is why you are going back to London?' He asked the question in a low, calm tone, yet for some reason it made a shiver of consternation race down her spine.

'Yes.'

'I don't think you've thought this out at all, Nicole,' he said furiously. 'How do you think you are going to manage on your own, with a baby and no job?'

'I'll get another job. No problem there.' She glared at him, her chin held high. 'I will be perfectly fine on my own.'

She probably *would* find herself another good job, Luke thought bleakly. He'd employ her again like a shot! He forced himself not to think like that. 'If you don't mind my saying so, that sounds very idealistic...and it is probably great in theory...but the reality is going to be very different, Nicole. And very difficult.'

'Don't lecture me, Luke. I'm the one having the morning sickness; I'm the one who can't even have a cup of coffee any more without wanting to throw up. I'm well aware of the realities.'

'No, you're not. This is just the start.' Luke's eyes raked over her face. 'This is the easy bit. You are going to be alone with a baby. You don't have a home. You don't have a job. Babies are expensive—they need feeding and clothing, not to mention all the necessary accessories. And if you are going to go back to work full-time it'll be very tiring. Who will help you when the baby cries at night and you are so bone-weary you feel you can't drag yourself out of bed to look after him?'

'I'll manage perfectly well—'

He cut across her. 'Then there is the question of schooling, of giving him or her the best start in life. You'll have to do everything alone…*you* will have all the responsibility.'

'And I'll enjoy it,' she said mutinously. 'If you are trying to scare me, it's not working, Luke.'

'And one day your child will turn around and ask about his father. Then what will you say?'

'I'll say…' Nicole faltered.

'Yes?' Luke held her eyes with determination.

'I'll cross that bridge when I come to it, Luke,' she said crossly. 'It's years in the future, and as long as my child knows that he or she is loved that's all that matters.'

'Very commendable…'

'I don't want to listen to this negativity!' Nicole was furious now.

'I'm just pointing out that, contrary to popular belief, being a single parent is a tough job.'

'I know what you are doing, Luke. You're trying to jolt me into thinking about getting rid of my baby, but it's not working.' She tried to push past him but he put a hand on her arm and wouldn't let her go.

'If you don't mind, I've had enough of this. I want you to leave.' She stared up at him in fury.

'But I *do* mind.' In contrast to hers, his voice was perfectly calm.

'You see, this is *exactly* why I didn't want to tell you

about the baby in the first place!' Her voice was vehement. 'I knew you would be like this.'

'You haven't given me a chance to say what I think.'

'On the contrary—I've just listened to your opinions at length.' Her eyes flashed fire at him. 'I didn't expect you to be pleased…in fact I didn't expect anything from you… so I'm not disappointed. Now, please take your hand off my arm—you are hurting me.'

He released her immediately and watched as she rubbed her skin as she walked away.

'I'm sorry, Nicole. I didn't realise I was hurting you.' He ran an impatient hand through the darkness of his hair. 'But you can't just leave things like this.'

'Watch me,' she said firmly.

Their eyes clashed across the room.

'I want you to go,' she reiterated.

For a long moment he said nothing, just looked at her in a deeply contemplative way. 'I didn't mean to upset you.'

'I'm not in the slightest bit upset,' she said quickly, but even as she was fervently denying the fact she was aware that deep down inside she felt very emotional. 'I'm furious with you for speaking to me the way you did…but that's about it.'

'You can't blame me for being angry—'

'Yes, I can—because I haven't done anything wrong.' She held his gaze defiantly. 'I certainly didn't deliberately set out to get pregnant *with you*.'

Luke held that gaze for a moment, then shrugged. 'But the fact is you *are* carrying my baby—and I had to drag the information out of you.'

'Come on, Luke, it wouldn't have made a blind bit of difference to you if I'd told you directly. We would still have had that conversation about how you think I won't be able to manage. The fact is you want me to get rid of the baby. But I've got news for you, Luke. You are not in control of this situation. I am.'

She put her hand on her hip and met his eyes squarely. 'I am having this baby and I will manage just fine. So you don't need to concern yourself about it.'

Luke watched her through narrowed eyes. She probably would manage very well on her own. She was determined and clever and self-sufficient enough to manage anything. 'But the fact is I *am* concerned,' he said quietly.

'Only because this is not what you want! We could go round in circles like this all day. I want you to go.'

As Nicole turned to leave the room she suddenly felt dizzy, it was just a fleeting feeling, but she had to reach out and grab hold of the table.

'Are you OK?' Instantly Luke was by her side. And when she didn't answer him straight away he put a steadying arm around her shoulder. 'Come on, you better sit down. I'll help you through to the other room.'

'I'm OK, Luke.' She shrugged him away angrily. 'I'm not an invalid!'

'I know that, but you do look very pale.'

'Don't pretend that you give a damn, because I'm not that stupid!' She looked over at him, her eyes wide and glimmering a fierce gold-green.

'Of course I care about you!' His reply was instant and vehement. 'You know I do!' he added gently.

Their eyes met and she felt a deep pang of regret. Maybe he did care about her. But not enough. Not in the way she ached for him to care.

'Come on, let's get you onto the sofa.'

She flinched away from his helping hand. She couldn't bear for him to touch her. It just made the raw pain of wanting him all the worse.

'Just go away, Luke.'

He stepped back from her, an expression of deep consternation in his eyes. 'Shall I phone for a doctor?'

'Don't be ridiculous.' She looked over at him and despite everything she smiled. 'I know what's wrong with me…remember?'

He smiled back.

Suddenly she was aware of tears prickling at the back of her eyes. Furious with herself, she drew herself up and headed for the front door. 'You'd better go.'

Luke hesitated for a moment before following her.

'Are you going to be OK?'

'Of course.' She glared at him. 'I'll be wonderful.'

'Take the day off work tomorrow.' He paused by the door, his voice brisk and businesslike. 'And then, when you've rested, we'll talk. That way we'll both have had a chance to calm down and think logically about the situation.'

'I am thinking logically,' she told him quickly. 'And I'm not going to change my mind, Luke. I'm having this baby.'

'But we still need to talk about it.' He said the words tersely. 'I *am* involved in this, whether you like it or not!'

With that he turned and left.

CHAPTER TWELVE

NICOLE spent a sleepless night, tossing and turning, trying not to think about Luke. But scenes from their confrontation kept replaying through her mind. His accusation that she had used him just to have a baby! How dared he? She had been shocked to find she was pregnant…shocked and more than a little scared. Yes, it was something she wanted…but it was something she had given up on a long time ago, when her marriage had broken down.

Then there had been Luke's negative comments about how she wouldn't be able to cope with a baby on her own.

Sadness vied with anger inside her. She tried to focus on the angry thoughts; it seemed easier to cope that way. She couldn't wait to get away from him, she told herself firmly. But even so she kept remembering his voice, and the look in his eyes as he'd told her that he cared about her. Her ex-husband had said something similar to her, she reminded herself. Just before he left her for another woman.

It was a relief when dawn broke and she could get up. Despite Luke's order that she take the day off, she got ready to go into work. She didn't want to sit around thinking about things. It was better to keep busy. So, almost in a defiant mood, she showered and dressed in a pale pink dress that skimmed her figure in a flattering way.

She scanned her appearance critically before leaving the apartment. Her hair was sitting perfectly, and even though she hadn't slept much she looked pretty good. She ran a hand soothingly down over the flatness of her stomach. It was still hard to believe that she was pregnant. A quiver of excitement cut through her anxiety about Luke. It didn't matter what he said…nothing could take away the pleasure of the fact that she was having a baby.

With a smile, she picked up her briefcase and headed into work.

Molly looked surprised when she walked into Nicole's office and saw her. 'I thought you were taking the day off!'

'What gave you that idea?'

'Luke just sent me a memo telling me you would be off for at least a week.'

'Did he?' Nicole felt a prickle of annoyance. 'We've obviously just got our wires crossed. I've no intention of taking time off.' She reached for the pile of mail waiting for her in the in-tray. 'Hold all my calls for a couple of hours, will you, Molly? I've still got some catching up with this paperwork from yesterday.'

'OK.' Molly smiled at her. 'You look better.'

'Actually, yes, I do feel better.' Nicole smiled as she suddenly realised she'd had no morning sickness today.

It was a hectic morning, as usual, and Nicole was glad of the fact—glad that she could bury herself in faxes and e-mails and not have to think about anything else.

At ten o' clock Molly put her head around the door. 'Luke is on the phone. Shall I put him through?'

Nicole hesitated. Part of her wanted to say no…but then Luke might think that she was hiding away from him. She needed to brazen this out as best she could, she told herself. 'Yes, put him through.'

With a supreme effort of will Nicole snatched up the phone and forced herself to sound briskly businesslike. 'Good morning, Luke, what can I do for you?'

'Now *there* is a loaded question!' He sounded amused.

Nicole had expected him to sound annoyed. She'd been unprepared for that deeply attractive husky tone.

'I thought I told you to take today off?' he continued.

'Luke, if I feel I need some time off I'll ask you for it,' she answered calmly. As she was speaking to him she filled in a report, trying to distract herself from thinking…from feeling.

'You are very stubborn,' he muttered. 'How are you feeling this morning?'

'Absolutely fine, thank you.'

'So, no sickness today, then?'

She tapped her pen impatiently against the desk. 'No, I told you, I feel great.'

'And no dizzy turns? I was worried about you after I left last night.'

Nicole frowned… Like hell he was. She wasn't going to be taken in by this note of concern. She knew damn well that his main worry was probably the fact that she was going to go through with this pregnancy.

'No. Now, I really better go. I've got someone waiting for me on the other line—'

'I'm going to book a restaurant for us to have lunch. So make sure you keep a few hours free from twelve-thirty onwards.'

'I'm not going to have lunch with you, Luke,' she said firmly.

'Yes, you are.' His voice was equally firm. 'I've come to a decision, Nicole, and we need to talk about it. I'll meet you down in the lobby at twelve-thirty.'

The line went dead. What did he mean, he had come to a decision? Nicole put the phone down with a frown. There were no decisions for him to make. She was leaving and she was having the baby.

She tried to concentrate on her work but it was difficult now. That sentence kept rolling through her mind. Maybe he was going to give her the name of some abortion clinic? Her mouth tightened in an angry line. Well, whatever he was going to say, she supposed she would have to meet him.

By the time twelve-thirty came around, Nicole was feeling extremely uneasy. She checked her appearance in her vanity mirror and reapplied her lipstick. Then, picking up her purse, she strolled towards the lifts. It would do Luke good to be kept waiting, she told herself. She wanted him to know that *she* was in control of this situation.

Even though Nicole had given herself a stern pep-talk about how she didn't care what Luke thought, and how she just wanted to be far away from him, her emotions seemed to give a weird flip of pleasure as she saw him standing in the lobby waiting for her.

He was just too handsome for any woman's peace of mind, she thought as her eyes drifted over the lightweight suit he was wearing. Not only did he dress stylishly, he had a fantastic body as well.

'I was just starting to think you weren't going to show.' He turned and smiled at her.

He also had the sexiest eyes of any man she had ever met, she thought distractedly.

'Well, I've got to eat.' She shrugged and tried to keep her voice flippant. 'So I thought I might as well listen to what you had to say.'

'Good decision.' There was a mocking gleam in his dark eyes which made her think that if she hadn't come down here he'd have gone up to her office and collected her physically.

Trying to ignore that disturbing mental picture, she turned to walk outside with him.

Luke's silver Porsche was parked directly outside and he had left the roof down. 'I thought we might as well get a few rays of sunshine while we are out.' He opened the passenger door for her and watched as she settled herself comfortably in the deep leather seat.

After the air-conditioned cool of the office, it was pleasant to sit in the sun, with a gentle breeze wafting over her as they drove down towards South Beach.

'You look lovely, by the way.' He glanced over at her as they stopped at traffic lights.

'Thanks.' She tried not to be pulled into the dark seductiveness of his gaze. Luke found it very easy to be charming, and she didn't want to allow herself to be lulled into a false sense of security.

'Did you sleep well last night?' he asked nonchalantly.

'Luke, will you just drop this phony interest in my well-being? It's annoying me now,' she said tightly as she looked away from him again.

'I'm asking because I am genuinely concerned for your health…and the baby's health,' he added softly.

She glanced back at him with a frown.

'Don't look at me with that suspicious light in your eyes.' His lips twisted in a mocking smile. 'I'm not an ogre, you know.'

'I never said you were.' Her heart twisted painfully. 'But I know you are not concerned about the baby.'

'That's a bit harsh, Nicole.' He changed gears and accelerated away from the lights with a grim expression on his face. 'I admit that maybe I could have handled the news that you are pregnant better. But it did come as a bit of a shock.'

Her swirling feeling of suspicion grew inside. Luke sounded conciliatory, and that wasn't usual.

'It came as a shock to me as well.'

'I know.' He nodded. 'I shouldn't have flown off the handle and accused you of deliberately getting pregnant… it was wrong of me.' He glanced across at her.

Something about the way he had said those words…the way he'd looked at her…made her feel incredibly vulnerable somehow. But she knew he was probably just trying to soften her up so that she would agree to whatever he wanted. She'd seen him in action enough times to know that he was very clever at getting his own way and that she shouldn't underestimate him! Nor should she underestimate the power he seemed to hold over her senses either. Because, at the same time as she was telling herself these things, she was drawn by that silky note of gentleness.

'Well, let's just forget about that, shall we?' she said hurriedly. 'I know you don't particularly trust women, so I suppose it was grist for the mill.'

He frowned, and seemed to think about that for a moment.

'I suppose you are right. I do have trust issues.' He shrugged. 'And, from what you told me yesterday, so do you.'

'I don't know what you are talking about,' she said firmly.

'Come on, Nicole. You told me about your ex-husband, remember?'

'That's all in the past—'

'Yes, and the past is what shapes us, isn't it?' He glanced over at her with a raised eyebrow. 'You know, sometimes I used to look at you and see this really vulnerable light in your eyes. I used to wonder about it…used to wonder if I had imagined it. But now I know I didn't.'

She shifted uncomfortably in her seat. 'Luke, this has nothing to do with our situation now—'

'Yes, it does.' Luke pulled the car over to the side of the road. 'You've been hurt a lot, and I certainly don't want to add to that.'

'You won't—because I won't let you!' she assured him crisply.

He smiled as he met her gaze. 'Maybe it's time we both lowered our barriers a little,' he said softly. 'We don't just have ourselves to think about now. There's a child involved.'

Luke could see the wariness in her eyes as she looked across at him. 'Come on, let's go and get something to eat,' he suggested lightly. 'We can talk honestly, try and relax a bit…OK?'

Nicole found herself nodding. OK, she would try and lower her barriers a little, she told herself. But not too much…Luke had too powerful an effect on her for her to risk that. If she weren't careful he would be taking over. The thought made apprehension spiral inside her.

Luke got out of the car and gave his keys to the valet attendant. Then, putting a hand at her back, he allowed her to precede him up onto the pavement. The restaurants at this point on the promenade were lined up together, and tables and chairs spilled out over the pavements under brightly colored awnings.

The buildings were all Art Deco in design, and the whole ambience was one of stylish sophistication.

Luke led her towards a restaurant that had its own courtyard garden. A band was playing salsa music at the back, and a few couples were dancing next to the swimming pool.

They sat under the shade of a parasol amidst a riot of greenery. Nicole had a clear view out across the road towards the wide sweep of white beach.

A waiter came over and Luke ordered drinks.

'Just a mineral water for me.' She smiled at the waiter and accepted the menu that was passed across to her.

As she glanced down at it she tried to pretend that she was interested in the food. But really all she could wonder about was why Luke had insisted on taking her out to lunch…and what motive lay behind that charmingly laid-back smile that he flashed across at her as their eyes met.

'It's lovely here.' She tried to relax a little.

'Yes…' Luke leaned back in his chair and his eyes drifted over her contemplatively.

'And the band is good.' She tried not to be aware of his gaze on her and instead looked over towards where the group were playing.

'The music reminds me of the first evening I took you out,' he said suddenly. 'Do you remember?'

'Yes, of course.' She smiled. 'We had dinner together

and then on the spur of the moment had a few dances at that Cuban salsa club next door to the restaurant.'

'Considering neither of us could dance, we did pretty well.'

Nicole laughed. 'Well, there were so many people on that small dance floor and the place was so dark it didn't really matter, did it?'

For a second she had a flashback to that evening. She remembered how they had laughed, and how in the end Luke had just taken her into his arms and they had smooched the night away. She had been oblivious to the crowds after that; all she had been aware of was his hard, lean body next to hers, the touch of his hands against her skin. She had hardly been able to wait until they could get out of the place so they could be alone together.

Their eyes met across the table, and she felt herself blush with the heat from that memory.

'We've always had good fun together,' he said softly.

'Yes…' Nicole looked away from him. She was relieved when the waiter brought their drinks at that moment. Remembering good times wouldn't help now, she told herself.

As soon as they were left alone again she quickly tried to switch the conversation onto safer ground. 'By the way, did you have a chance to look into the problem with that contract I mentioned yesterday?'

'We are not talking business this afternoon, Nicole,' he said firmly. 'It's off-limits.'

Her eyes narrowed on him for a moment. 'Well, I was only asking—'

'Save work for the office.' He cut across her briskly. 'We have more important things to concentrate on.'

'More important than work?' She couldn't help the sarcastic note that crept into her voice. 'You must be worried, Luke. Because in my experience *nothing* is more important than business where you are concerned.'

'Well, maybe...like yours...my priorities have just been given a good shake-up.'

'I'm sorry for that, Luke,' she flared. 'I certainly didn't mean to shake up your well-ordered world—'

'No, you just meant to run away without telling me the truth.'

She glared at him, her heart thumping rapidly against her chest.

The waiter arrived at that moment to ask if they were ready to place their food order. Nicole looked back towards the menu. The atmosphere was tense and horrible now, and she wasn't in the slightest bit hungry. This situation was too uncomfortable...She chose the first thing off the menu. All she wanted to do was get this lunch over and get away.

Luke, on the other hand, took a little more time over his selection, and chatted amiably with the waiter.

He was too relaxed, Nicole thought suddenly. She had observed him in times of conflict over business and had found that the more laid-back he seemed the more on your guard you had to be...because there was usually some surprise plan waiting around the corner.

The notion made her very uneasy. Nicole reached for her glass of water and took a sip. She was starting to become paranoid, she told herself sensibly. What plan could he possibly have? *She* was in the driving seat. This was her baby, and he couldn't make her do anything she didn't want to.

'You seem very on edge, Nicole,' Luke remarked as they were left alone again.

'I suppose that's because I *am* on edge. I know you are not happy with this situation…and I'm wondering why you've invited me here. Maybe we should just cut to the bottom line and you can tell me,' she said shakily.

'I've told you what I want. I want us to talk honestly.' He held her eyes steadily. 'And I don't want us to fall out.'

'That's easier said than done.'

'Not if we meet each other halfway.'

'Halfway?'

'Yes, and sort things out in a cordial fashion.'

'You make this sound like just another business deal gone awry.' Her lips twisted in a half-smile.

'I was hoping we could agree on things without becoming too emotional.'

There it was again. That pragmatic, relaxed tone…

'God forbid we become emotional,' Nicole grated sarcastically. 'That would go completely against everything you stand for, wouldn't it, Luke?'

She watched his eyes darken angrily. 'I mean I don't want us to argue. I was trying to be civilised.'

'You weren't being very civilised yesterday, when you told me I wouldn't be able to bring up a child on my own.'

'I said it would be difficult,' he corrected her quickly. 'And anyway, I thought we'd agreed to put yesterday behind us.'

She shrugged, and glared at him mutinously. 'I just hope you are not going to mention the word *termination,* Luke. Because I'm going to get up and leave if you do—'

There was a look of horror in Luke's eyes now. 'You really think I'd say something like that to you?'

'I thought…' She brushed a hand unsteadily through her hair. 'I don't know, Luke…'

'God, no!' He looked over at her earnestly. 'Nicole, can we start again?' he asked suddenly, his voice husky. 'This conversation isn't going quite as I'd planned.'

For a second she was completely disarmed by that tone in his voice and that look in his eye. 'What way had you planned it?' she asked shakily.

'Oh, I don't know.' He shook his head. 'I've been awake all night, thinking.' He reached across and took hold of her hand.

The touch of his fingers against her skin set her pulses racing in chaotic disorder.

'You have?' Nicole looked at him in surprise. Luke never lost sleep about anything.

'Yes.' He met her gaze firmly then. 'And I'm worried about you.'

'Worried!' She felt a jolt of disappointment and pulled her hand away from his. She didn't want him to be worried about her!

'Nicole, I can't let you go back to London and deal with this on your own.'

'Well, you are just going to have to, Luke.' She didn't know how she kept her voice so calm, because inside she was a seething mass of furious regret. 'Because I don't *need* you to worry about me!' She glared at him.

'Maybe not…but I am just the same.' He raked a hand distractedly through his hair.

'I can assure you that I will be fine.'

'You can't assure me of anything, Nicole,' he said harshly. 'You are running away back to England!'

'I'm not running away!' She sat straighter in her chair. 'I'm thinking about what is best for my child.'

'*Our* child,' he corrected her quietly.

Nicole looked across at him, her emotions racing wildly.

'I've thought about it long and hard,' he said softly. 'And I can't let you go. This child is my responsibility as well as yours. I want you to stay here in Miami with me.'

CHAPTER THIRTEEN

FOR a long moment Nicole was so stunned that she couldn't find her voice to answer him. Luke, however, didn't seem to notice. He was talking about the fact that they were both responsible for this precious new life and they had a duty to do their very best for it.

It was the word *duty* that finally snapped her back into some kind of sanity. 'I'm sorry. But this isn't going to work.'

Luke had been in the middle of telling her that in his opinion a child needed two parents. He trailed off and looked at her through narrowed eyes. 'What's not going to work?'

'This.' She waved a hand airily between them. 'This show of…of concern is all very noble. But I am not hanging around in Miami while you salve your suddenly acquired new conscience and play duty dad. So you can just forget it!'

Luke shook his head. 'You misunderstand, Nicole. I'm not trying to salve my conscience. I want to do my best for this child. I want to make sure that you are financially secure. I want to look after you.'

'And I don't want to be looked after.' She cut across him coolly. 'You know, Luke, when my ex-husband was leaving me he told me that his new girlfriend was pregnant. He also told me that he still had feelings for me. That he didn't really want to leave. But he felt that he had to do the right thing by his child.'

'Nicole, I know you've been hurt, but this situation is different.'

'No, it's not. Because do you know what I felt when he said those things?' She fixed him with a clear and penetrating gaze. 'I felt sympathy for his girlfriend…and I thought that if she had an ounce of sense she would send him packing as soon as he landed on her doorstep.'

'Would you have had him back?'

Her eyes opened wide. 'You must be joking! I wouldn't have had Patrick back if he'd been gift-wrapped.'

Luke smiled. 'Good. Because he sounds like a complete jerk—'

'Whereas *you* sound absolutely so damn perfect?' She looked over at him and shook her head. 'Luke, I've got news for you. I don't want a father for my baby who is just sticking by us out of duty.'

'But I've thought about it, and it's what I want to do,' Luke said seriously.

'I'm sure it is right at this moment. But it won't work. What are you going to do? Take an hour off every week to bounce the baby on your knee and then run back to your precious business for your real commitment?'

'I think I can do better than that.' Luke's voice was terse.

'And how's a baby going to fit in to that contemporary hi-tech apartment of yours? Not to mention the fact that it's going to play havoc with your social life. And do you think a baby seat will fit in the back of that Porsche?'

'Very funny,' he grated.

'Yes, it is—isn't it?' Nicole held his dark gaze for a moment. 'Because the truth is that after a few months of playing duty dad you'd be bored to tears. The baby would get in the way of your jet-set lifestyle and your glamorous women.'

'You are wrong about that, Nicole,' Luke said quietly.

'No, I'm not.' She took a deep breath. 'But you were right about one thing. We are both products of our past. I'm older and wiser and I'm certainly not going to get tied… however tenuously…to the wrong man again. And you…' She met his eyes steadily. 'You are an emotional desert, Luke.'

Before Luke could say anything to that she was pushing her chair away from the table. 'Thanks for the invitation to lunch, but I think I've just lost my appetite.'

'Nicole, don't go!' But he was talking to himself. She was walking away from him, out onto the street.

Luke wanted to rush after her, but at that second the waiter arrived with their food. He was forced to waste precious minutes trying to explain that they wouldn't now be eating and asking to have the bill. By the time he followed Nicole out of the restaurant there was no sign of her.

Fury rushed through his entire body as he glanced up and down the crowded street and then across the road towards the beach. He had made a complete and utter botch of everything. With a grim feeling of utter frustration he took out his mobile phone, brought up Nicole's number and dialled it.

Nicole had planned to jump into a cab and dash back to the office. But when she got outside the restaurant she suddenly couldn't face going back to work. Instead she found herself crossing the road and walking back in the direction they had come, cutting across a strip of parkland towards the beach.

She sat on a wall and looked out across the wide sweep of white sand. It was a perfect day. The sun was beating down from a clear blue sky and the waves were crashing in against the shore, with just a hint of a breeze rustling through the palm trees.

Would she never learn? Nicole wondered angrily. For a while, when Luke had looked at her across that table and made it clear that he wanted their baby, she had felt a rush of happiness that had almost overwhelmed her. In those precious few seconds she had pictured them as a couple… as a family. It was amazing how many pictures of the future you could fit into a few seconds…and how blissful those images could be. Blissful—but foolish!

As if Luke could ever be a family man!

Her phone rang, and she took it out of her handbag and flipped it open. Luke's name was flashing on the screen.

She disconnected and put the phone back in her bag again. There was no point talking.

But what about the fact that he wants to try and do the right thing? a little voice cut through her unhappiness. Didn't that count for something? Did she really have the right to make the decision to march off back to London? They had made this baby together…it wasn't just her decision to take…was it?

She swallowed hard on a lump in her throat. But how could she stay here knowing that she loved him? Watching him play dad at a distance would be torturous. For the preservation of her sanity she needed to leave.

The phone rang again. It would be him…she knew it would be him. She tried to ignore it.

Would allowing him to play dad at a distance be better than nothing at all? That persistent little voice inside her was rising in volume, cutting through all her strong thoughts.

She fished the phone out of her bag again and opened it. As she had known it would be, Luke's name was on the screen.

He would be a terrible dad, she told herself. He'd always put business first…and he'd always have a different beautiful woman on his arm. And there lay the crux. Was she fleeing back to London because she couldn't face the fact that she wasn't going to be in his life? And, if so, was that selfish? Shouldn't she be putting her baby's needs first?

Maybe Luke would make a terrific dad! How did she know? Didn't Luke deserve a chance to prove himself?

The phone rang and rang, and suddenly she couldn't stand it any more and answered it.

'Nicole…thank God.' His voice was fervent. 'Look, I'm sorry. How can I put this right?'

The lump in her throat grew. This didn't sound like the Luke she knew.

'I don't know,' she murmured honestly.

'Where are you?' His husky voice tore at her emotions.

'I'm…I'm across the road…by the park.'

'OK, stay where you are. I'm on my way.'

With a frown, Nicole snapped the phone closed. This was probably a mistake. She was feeling vulnerable, and it wasn't a good idea to talk in this state. What she should have done was head back to the office and bury herself in work until she had regained some strength.

She put her phone away and stood up to leave—and that was when the first pain struck her in the stomach. She didn't dare to move for a moment, and she waited with apprehension to see if it would return. A few seconds later it was followed by another, sharper pain.

She sat back down on the wall and put a hand to her stomach in alarm.

'Nicole?'

She looked up and saw that Luke was beside her, but his voice seemed to be coming from a long way off. She felt dizzy now.

'Honey, are you OK?' He crouched down beside her and looked at her with concern.

'I think you'd better get me to the hospital,' she whispered, as another pain stabbed through her. She was really frightened now. This couldn't be happening! She was losing the baby…she could feel it… A sob rose in her throat.

Afterwards, the memory of getting to the hospital was all a bit of a blur to Nicole. She remembered that Luke had taken charge, and that his calm manner had been soothing. He had started to help her to walk and then, as the pain came back, he had swept her up into his arms and carried her.

In a matter of minutes he had hailed a passing cab.

Now Nicole was in a private room as a nurse took her details and they waited for a doctor. She couldn't believe that this was happening! She had felt so well this morning! Was it her fault? Had she done something wrong? Worked too hard? Maybe if she had taken the day off, as Luke suggested?

The doctor came into the room and spoke to her before

starting an examination. Nicole closed her eyes and prayed that her baby would be all right.

Luke was pacing up and down in the corridor outside. The smell of antiseptic and the bright neon lights dazzled him. He couldn't remember ever feeling this helpless before. Nicole had asked that he wait outside while they were examining her, and he had respected her wishes, but he just wanted to be with her, to do something.

He whirled around as the nurse came out of the room. 'How is she? Is the baby OK?'

The nurse looked over at him with sympathy. 'We don't know yet if Nicole has lost the baby. Dr Curran has suggested that we do an ultrasound scan to see exactly what is going on.'

'And how long will that take?' He frowned.

'Not long. There is a coffee machine at the other end of the corridor, and some comfortable seats if you'd like to wait down there,' she told him.

Luke shook his head. 'I'd like to be with Nicole while she is having the scan—'

'Yes, of course…Nicole has asked for you. I just meant for you to wait while Dr Curran is finishing the examination. Give us a few more minutes and then I'll bring you in.' She hurried away again, and once more he was left to pace up and down outside.

It felt like for ever before they told him he could go inside. Nicole was lying on the bed, propped up by a few pillows; she looked so fragile that his heart ached for her. Her hair was so dark against the pallor of her skin, and her large green eyes were misted with anxiety.

He went straight across to her and took hold of her hand.

Nicole was so glad to see him that she could feel tears welling up inside her.

'So, how is the patient doing, Dr Curran?' he asked.

'Nicole's pain has stopped, so that is something.' The doctor pushed her glasses further up her nose as she studied some notes. 'I am having difficulty finding the baby's heartbeat. But we'll know more when we do the ultrasound.' She put the notes down suddenly and looked over at them both with a serious expression on her face. 'I'm afraid miscarriages are common within the first weeks of pregnancy. It's a risky time.'

'Are you saying you think Nicole has lost the baby?' Luke's voice was grim.

'I'm saying that it's a possibility.' She looked from one to the other of them. 'I am sorry, but I feel I should prepare you for the worst…just in case.'

Nicole felt a lump rising in her throat. She wanted to cry, but the tears seemed lodged deep inside, like a dam waiting to burst.

'Are you going to do the ultrasound now?' Luke asked.

He sounded so calm, Nicole thought. Just like he did when he was in the office, sorting out an unexpected problem. She listened as he asked questions and the doctor explained the procedure.

'Thank you, Doctor.' Luke nodded.

'You're welcome.'

The door closed behind her and they were left alone.

'It doesn't sound good, does it?' Nicole's voice was shaky.

Luke perched on the side of the bed and looked at her gently. 'The doctor was just preparing us for the worst. But that doesn't mean the worst has happened.'

'I don't want to lose my baby, Luke.' She whispered the words unsteadily. 'I want this child so much…'

'I know, honey.' He stroked her hair back from her face with a gentle hand. 'But let's think positively.'

She noticed how ashen his face was, how his eyes were filled with an intensity of pain. She had never seen Luke look like that before, and it shook her. Suddenly she realised that he was trying to keep calm for her, and that this was tearing him apart too!

Tears trickled down her face as she realised that he was hurting every bit as much as she was.

'Don't cry, Nicole!' He put an arm around her, and the next moment she was pulled close against his chest. 'Let's remain positive about our baby, hmm…? Let's not cross bridges until we have to.'

His voice was husky and deep and infinitely soothing. She leaned against him, grateful for the support, loving the feeling of closeness, the familiar tang of his cologne…the warmth of his body. She closed her eyes and tried to draw strength from him. 'Luke, I'm so sorry.'

'Sorry for what?' He stroked her hair tenderly. 'You haven't done anything wrong.'

'I said horrible things to you at lunch!' She squeezed her eyes tightly closed.

'I think I deserved them.'

'No, you didn't!' She pulled back and looked at him through eyes that burnt with feeling. 'You told me you wanted our baby, and I…I didn't realise just how much you meant it!'

'Yes, I did mean it. But I can understand you being wary of my motives. After all, I have always enjoyed life in the fast lane, without commitments.' He shook his head ruefully. 'You're right about me. I have been an emotional desert.'

'I really shouldn't have said that,' she murmured.

'Yes, you should—because it's the truth.' He took hold of her hands. 'And I've deliberately tried to keep myself that way as well…it seemed safer, somehow.'

'I know that feeling.' She bit down on her lip. 'I felt the same after my marriage broke up. Told myself that I wasn't going to get emotionally involved ever again.'

'Yes, but you are a nicer person than me. Because you couldn't keep that way of life up. You are warm and loving and you wanted more—which is why you finished with me. And I don't blame you, Nicole.' His lips twisted ruefully. 'I've been so blind… I just didn't see the truth… Or maybe I just didn't want to see the truth until it hit me.'

Nicole swallowed hard. 'And now you realise how much you want to be a father…that you're ready for that commitment—'

'Not just that…'

She looked at him with puzzled eyes.

'Nicole, from the first moment you walked into my office you changed my life.'

'I did?'

He nodded, and wiped a tear away from her face with a tender hand. 'I thought I had my life all in order until the day you walked into my office and into my life, with your fabulous green eyes and your fiery spirit. I was totally…totally captivated. And since that day everything I thought I knew about myself has been thrown into chaos.'

'It has?' Nicole was looking at him in bewilderment.

He nodded. 'Oh, I've tried to pretend that it hasn't…in

fact I've been too cussedly stubborn to even listen to my own heart! When you finished things I was devastated. But I told myself it was just an affair and I'd get over it….and then I realised that I wasn't just going to get over it.' He gave a grim laugh. 'And when you told me that you wanted a deeper and more meaningful relationship I was quite frankly in a complete tailspin.'

She smiled shakily.

'I've accused you of wanting to run away back to London. But *I've* been the one who has been running away, Nicole…' His voice held a deep, raw sincerity that touched her to the core. 'I've been running away from my own emotions, running away from myself… And when you put in your resignation I realised that. I was devastated at the thought that I'd lost you. Because without you I'm nothing. You make me a better person…you make my life complete…'

Her heart lurched crazily and she just couldn't find her voice to say anything.

'And then I found out you were pregnant. I was in a state of shock…not only because I'd found out I couldn't bear to lose you…but suddenly I found that I wanted the whole package. I want you and the baby…and I want it so much that it hurts.'

She swallowed down her tears.

'This is what I meant to say to you over lunch. But of course old habits die hard and I found myself hiding behind all kinds of excuses to keep you here…' He shook his head. 'And now look at me…blurting all this out at the wrong time. I have made a complete mess of things.'

'It's not the wrong time.' Her voice was groggy with tears.

'It is. But I'm going to say it anyway… I love you, Nicole, and I think I have from the first moment I set eyes on you. I've just been too stupid and too stubborn to face it. And now I can't face the thought of life without you. If we lose our baby…' His voice cracked slightly and he smiled. 'Sorry…I just need you so much, Nicole, and I'm begging you to give me a chance to prove myself to you. I want us to face this situation as a couple…'

Nicole put her arms around him and just held him. 'I want that too.' She whispered the words fervently. 'More than you'll ever know.'

'Really?' He pulled back from her. 'Because I know that before you found out you were pregnant you wanted to get out of our relationship and find someone else…someone who didn't have all my hang-ups…'

'I want *you*, Luke…' Her heart was thundering against her chest. 'That's why I finished things. Because I love you and I didn't think you would ever return that love.'

She saw the look of hope in his eyes. 'So…no matter what the outcome of this scan is…we'll face it together?'

She nodded.

'Nicole, will you marry me?'

Nicole was so stunned that she couldn't say anything for a moment. 'Luke, I—'

'Don't say no!' He placed a finger over her lips. 'I know this is the wrong time, but I have to say this now. I love you so much. Just give me a chance to prove to you that my feelings are genuine.' He watched as a tear trickled down her cheek.

'Don't cry, sweetheart, please. It just breaks my heart.'

'You shouldn't be saying this.'

'I know. But if our baby is all right and I ask you later, it will seem like I'm only asking you because we are having a child. And if the news is bad…God forbid…' His voice was grim now. 'Well, at least something good will have come out of this situation.'

'Luke, you don't know what you are saying.' Her voice was husky with the weight of her emotion. 'If we've lost this baby you might be committing yourself to someone who can never give you a family. I couldn't get pregnant with Patrick…this child might be my last chance.'

'We'll take that a day at a time, Nicole…a step at a time.'

She shook her head. 'I can't marry you, Luke. I'm sorry, but I can't go through all that again.' Her voice cracked huskily. 'I can't go through the pain of not being able to give you what you want. I've been through that once before with Patrick, and it was…unbearable…' She looked up at him with wide eyes. 'I suppose that was the reason I tried to keep my emotions switched off when we started our affair. I was scared of falling in love all over again, scared of the same thing happening…'

'The same thing *isn't* going to happen—because I'm not Patrick,' he said gently. 'And I love you.' He gripped hold of her shoulders and looked at her. 'I love you…I need you…and as long as I have you I can face anything else.'

'And you still want me even though…if I lose this baby…I might not be able to give you another one?' She looked up at him with wide green eyes.

'I want you with all my heart, Nicole,' he murmured. 'And if we lose this child we'll face it together…comfort each other…grieve together…and then try again—maybe adopt. There are ways around the situation.'

She shook her head. 'I can't think about this now, Luke,' she said brokenly.

Luke hesitated. He wanted to press her further, but she looked so distraught. 'OK…we'll leave it for now.' He wrapped his arms around her and for a moment they just held each other. 'Just know that I'm here for you.' He stroked her hair. 'And I always will be. No matter what.'

His words made her melt.

The door opened and the nurse came in.

'It's time to take you down for your scan now, Nicole.'

The fear instantly returned, but Luke caught hold of her hand. She could feel his strength and his love in that touch, and it helped.

Nicole would never forget those next few moments as they wheeled her through to another room and a different doctor appeared and introduced herself.

There was silence as the doctor started the procedure. Nicole looked at the expressions on the doctor's face as she looked at the screen that would show her baby.

'Is everything OK, Doctor?' It was Luke who asked the question, and his voice was tense.

The doctor didn't answer straight away; she was too busy staring at the screen. Then she smiled. 'I can see your baby…and, yes, everything appears to be fine.'

Nicole hadn't realised how hard she had been holding her emotions in check until then; she felt weak with relief and just buried her face in her hands.

Luke reached and took her into his arms. 'It's OK, honey…everything is going to be all right now.'

The doctor smiled at Luke as she got up from her seat beside them and left them alone.

EPILOGUE

A WARM fragrant breeze drifted across the turquoise water of the Gulf of Mexico and rustled the palm trees outside the bedroom window.

Nicole stood and watched as the early-morning sun played over the water. She loved being down on the Florida Keys.

'What are you thinking about?' Luke's voice jolted her from her contemplation.

'Just how lovely it is here…' She looked around at her husband, who was lying in the four-poster bed; the sheets were low on his abdomen, showing his fabulous torso to advantage. Nicole felt a flare of desire just looking at him.

'I thought you were asleep.' She smiled.

'No, I was lying here admiring your sexy silhouette in that white nightdress.'

She blushed and he laughed. 'Amazing—I can still make you blush even after twelve months of marriage…happy anniversary, darling.' He held out a hand to her and she went back to bed, slipping in beside him to melt into his arms.

'Happy anniversary.' She kissed him, and for a long time they were lost in each other's embrace as passion flared.

'I love you so much.' She breathed the words against his

skin. 'And I just want to say thank you for a wonderful year…' She pressed her lips against his chest and kissed him fiercely.

'Hey, it's just the start of many wonderful years to come.' He squeezed her closer. 'Marrying you was the best deal I ever closed.'

She looked at him wryly and he laughed. 'I don't mind saying that you were the hardest deal to break as well.' He shook his head. 'Negotiations have never been so tough.'

Nicole laughed. She had made Luke wait for a while into her pregnancy before capitulating to marriage. It hadn't been that she was trying to play hard to get, or being deliberately difficult. She had just been wary of marriage. Living with Luke would have suited her.

But Luke had pursued her with dogged determination. He had sent her flowers and gifts and declared his undying love, and had told her that nothing less than total commitment would satisfy him.

She smiled to herself now as she thought about the change in Luke. They had almost had a role reversal after his declaration of love. She'd been the wary one and he'd been so…sure.

'You didn't need to send me all those presents…' She kissed him now. 'Because the best thing you ever did was to give me Thomas.' She whispered the words huskily.

As if on cue their baby gave a gurgling cry in the cot next to the bed. They both rolled over to look in at him.

Thomas Santana was ten months old now, and was the most beautiful baby boy. He had jet-dark hair and eyes like Luke's and he had a smile and a sunny nature that melted their hearts.

'Hello, my darling.' Nicole sat up and reached over to pick him up and bring him into the bed between them.

Every day when she woke and looked at Thomas she marvelled at her little miracle, and gave thanks for the fact that although it had been a difficult pregnancy she'd had Luke by her side, supporting her and being strong for her.

'So, what shall we do today?' she asked. 'A bit of gardening, perhaps, or—?'

'Never mind the garden…' Luke said firmly. 'You, me and Thomas are off to Barbados this afternoon, for two sun-drenched and relaxing weeks.'

Nicole looked at him in surprise. Luke had been due to go back up to Miami first thing tomorrow, leaving her here at the Key West house. 'I thought you had some important meetings lined up at the office this week?'

He smiled at her. 'I've delegated.'

'Have you?' Nicole grinned. 'These really are changed days!'

'Well, we never did get around to going away for our honeymoon, did we?'

Nicole shook her head. They'd had to cancel their trip because she had been ordered to take things easy for the rest of her pregnancy and it had meant a lot of bed-rest.

'And, as I recall, at the time I did promise you a golden beach and as much ice cream as you can eat…and a promise is a promise, Mrs Santana…'